A Different Kind of Reunion

by

Joanne Guidoccio

A Gilda Greco Mystery

A Different Kind of Reunion

Cover Art by Kim Mendoza

The Wild Rose Press, Inc.
PO Box 708
Adams Basin, NY 14410-0708
Visit us at www.thewildrosepress.com

Publishing History
First Mainstream Mystery Edition, 2018
Print ISBN 978-1-5092-2038-0
Digital ISBN 978-1-5092-2039-7

A Gilda Greco Mystery
Published in the United States of America

Jim whistled.

"You sure don't like it easy. With all your millions, you'd think this crap could somehow miss landing on you. But you do seem to attract it." He chuckled. "Might be something to address with a therapist or maybe the psychic you've just met."

"I didn't just meet her. I got to know her and her parents very well during those seven months I taught in Parry Sound. They're good people." While I was also skeptical, I did feel the urge to defend her. She had been so sincere and so open. I couldn't fathom the notion of Cassandra faking or putting on the airs of a psychic. It wasn't in her nature to be deceitful.

"I'm sure they are," Jim said. "But let's face some facts here. Most psychics need to make a living. I don't doubt this lady has some intuitive ability—as many women do—but I don't think it's enough to catch a murderer. The constable is grasping at straws. What did you say his name was?"

"Leo. Leo Mulligan."

"Tall, dark-haired guy. Good-looking and a bit of a rascal."

"He's evolved." I immediately regretted my response. Knowing Jim, he would pounce and tease me.

"And you're interested," Jim said, chuckling. "What does your boyfriend think about this cozy reunion you're having?"

Dedication

To my former students…
You have enriched my life beyond measure

Acknowledgments

To my family:
Tony, Augy, Ernie, Judy, Lilly, Joan,
Christina, Deanna, Olivia and Ava.
I appreciate your ongoing support and encouragement.
~*~

To the wonderful companions on my journey,
especially Patricia Anderson, Carla Barnes,
Cindy Carroll, Fil Derewianko, Dennis Fitter,
Luke Hill, Sandy and Jim Hill, Brenda McGinnis,
Magda Viehover, and Cathy Whyte.
~*~

To my fellow Guelph Partners in Crime: Alison Bruce,
Gloria Ferris, Liz Lindsay, and Donna Warner. I enjoy
our meetups and traveling show.
~*~

To Editor Ramona DeFelice Long.
I appreciate your professionalism
and wonderful insights.
Molte grazie!
~*~

To the librarians and support staff at
the Guelph Public Library,
especially Laura Baker, Karen Cafarella, Andrea Curtis,
Deb Quaile, Robin Tunney, and Henry Wiebe.
~*~

To Kinan Werdski, Rhonda Penders,
and the dedicated people at The Wild Rose Press.
Thank you for making this book possible.

Chapter 1

Thursday, October 24, 2013

One missed email. While I couldn't be one hundred percent certain it was the only one I had ever overlooked, this omission would haunt me. And matters weren't helped when the cantankerous constable on the telephone said, "If you had read that email, Sarah McHenry might still be alive."

Leaning back in my recliner, I closed my eyes and tried to recall Sarah's face. But all I could see were curtains of blond hair or, more precisely, three sets of curtains of blond hair. The Barbies—Mean Barbie, Mellow Barbie, Moody Barbie—came to mind. How I had detested those nicknames and some of the more cruel ones the students tossed about like puffs of cotton candy, oblivious to the pain and potential scarring that could linger for decades and even lifetimes. I spent the first two weeks of my teaching stint calling out the children whenever they used those nicknames and giving detentions to anyone who persisted.

Moody Barbie. That had been Sarah's moniker. Prone to tears and bouts of the silent treatment, she often retreated into her own world. A budding artist, she would take out her sketch pad and draw whenever she finished her work or needed to separate herself from the others. Had she decided life was much too difficult and retreated even farther? That had been my first thought when Constable Mulligan read the infamous email: *We need your help.* But the use of the first-person plural pronoun conjured up another meaning, one even more sinister.

Who was in danger? Family members? The Barbies? Other classmates? Why reach out to me after more than two decades of silence? And how did she find my workplace email address? All these questions swirled through my mind, and I longed to ask for details. But I didn't want to anger the grief-stricken constable who was bemoaning the senseless way Sarah had died, alone and exposed to the cool autumn evening. A shocking occurrence, but even more so in Parry Sound.

With a population of about six thousand people, the northern Ontario town was often described as Friendly Sound, a community where everyone was related or connected. Best known as the home of hockey legend Bobby Orr, the town offered four seasons of sports and recreational activities—an athlete's paradise—and an easy camaraderie hard to find elsewhere. People mattered in Parry Sound.

Glancing at the article he sent, I noted the date of Sarah's death: September 30. Over three weeks had passed and Constable Mulligan was only now contacting me? "I'm surprised you didn't call earlier."

A long, drawn-out sigh followed. "I...well...we didn't find her for three days and—"

"Three days!" Had Sarah's parents and all her siblings moved away? What about her friends from her school days? Had no one noticed her missing?

"She had moved back into her parents' house, but

she treated it like a hotel. Her dad complained about her drinking and…uh…flings, but he did little to stop it. And her mother struggled to keep the peace."

Flings in Parry Sound? I shuddered at the thought of Sarah hopping from one man's bed to another in a small town where every deviation from the norm was analyzed to death. I also felt for her parents. What must they be thinking now? Could they have intervened and insisted that Sarah receive counseling?

I needed more details. "So you found the body and the cell phone around the third of October. Why did you—"

"Uh…not quite. One of the waitresses at the restaurant where Sarah worked found her phone a while back and stored it for safekeeping. The waitress forgot all about it until she decided to clean out her locker earlier this week."

More carelessness! And most of it due to Sarah's carelessness with her own life. Why was she drinking and behaving promiscuously? What was she doing on that hill in the middle of the night? So many questions I longed to ask, but I doubted the Constable would even know where to begin.

"Gilda…Gilda are you still there?" Annoyance crept into Constable Mulligan's voice.

"Sorry. I'm still trying to wrap my head around this tragedy." At age thirty-five, Sarah had so many unexplored and unrealized dreams. I recalled one dream concocted during her Grade Eight year: Sarah Ann McHenry moves to New York City and launches the SAM label, an upscale line of clothing for fashion-conscious women worldwide.

"You and everyone else in Parry Sound." He

paused. "You have no idea what kind of help she would need?"

"I'm sorry. I haven't seen Sarah in years." Over twenty years had passed since Grade Eight Graduation night. And that was the last time I saw Sarah, or any of the other students, for that matter. I decided not to share that statistic and further enrage Constable Mulligan.

"That's how it goes when outsiders breeze into our town," he said, raising his voice. "You're here for a good time, not a long time."

I bit my tongue and said nothing. While I had experienced many fulfilling moments during those seven months in Parry Sound, it wasn't easy. Determined to shove aside thoughts of my ex-husband and his gay lover, I put in ten-hour days and crawled into bed, too exhausted to do or think of anything else.

Luigi Battista. Another blast from the past. And one I had worked hard to put behind me. I couldn't and wouldn't let my mind wander back to that disastrous marriage. And then I recalled a subject line I had seen a while back. *Hi, Ms. Battista.* Was that Sarah's email? I archived it along with the ever-growing batch I planned to peruse at the month's end. In my mind, I had classified the email as non-urgent and a possible annoyance.

"Gilda, could you drop by tomorrow?" Constable Mulligan said, his voice cracking. "I'd like to wrap up this investigation as soon as possible. Give her parents some closure."

Did he think he could wrap it up in a day? And what on earth could I contribute to the investigation? It didn't make any sense at all. "Uh...I'm sorry. I'm having trouble with all of this. I don't know—"

He cleared his throat. "We could meet for lunch at Trapper's Choice Restaurant. They have fresh pickerel on Fridays."

"I have clients scheduled for appointments all afternoon." Or most of the afternoon. I liked to close the ReCareering office early on Friday afternoons.

"You're still working?" he asked, surprise overtaking his previous gruffness. "I didn't think you'd need to…I mean, you should be okay…"

He knew about my lottery win. Not surprising, since the lottery people had plastered my name and face everywhere when I won nineteen million dollars in Lotto 649. A quick Google search would have revealed my four-year-old lottery win. Old news, but still there on the second and third pages.

Tempted to end the conversation, I realized I couldn't turn my back on Sarah or any of the others who might still be in danger. The use of the pronoun "we" suggested more deaths might follow. Or I could be over-thinking Sarah's motivation for sending the email. It could have been a simple request for money. Since winning the lottery, I had heard from many friends and acquaintances who suddenly needed quick influxes of cash. But if Sarah had heard of my lottery win, she would have known to send the email to Gilda Greco not Gilda Battista.

I mentally scanned my calendar. I had a two o'clock appointment and would be free to leave around three. I calculated the distance and figured I could drive to Parry Sound in ninety minutes or so. I added an extra hour and shared my plans.

"Great! You'll have a couple of hours before the séance."

"What séance?" Were Friday night séances a regular occurrence in Parry Sound? And why would someone like Constable Mulligan, who didn't sound like a touchy-feely type of guy, attend one?

A low laugh escaped him. "I'm not losing it, Gilda. At least, not yet." He paused. "Cassandra Coburn is participating in a holistic fair here in town, and she's agreed to help us out."

"You hired a psychic?" I didn't think a small town like Parry Sound could afford the services of one of Canada's best-known psychics. Last fall, Cassandra was a keynote speaker at a fundraiser for breast cancer in Sudbury. Unfortunately, I was away and didn't attend. But the other career counselors in the office had raved about her insights and intuitive abilities.

"You've lost touch." Another drawn-out sigh came down the wire. "Cassandra was a student in your class. She was Sandra Maddalone back then."

"Really?" Pretty and plump with long, curly black hair. And the only Italian in the class. Her parents had befriended me and invited me to monthly dinners at their home. They would have invited me more often, but I didn't want to impose on their kindness. They also connected with my parents and godparents in Sudbury.

After leaving Parry Sound, I stayed in touch for several years, but the letters soon trickled into cards, and eventually no contact. Until their tragic deaths. A car accident where both parents died, and Sandra survived. I found out too late to attend the funeral but did send a Mass card. I tried to connect with Sandra, but she was still in the hospital. Deep in a life-threatening coma, she couldn't even attend her parents' funeral. All of this I heard from my godmother, Maria, who maintained a correspondence with Sandra's aunt.

New name and surname. Coburn rang a bell. Two boys came to mind—twins. Fraternal twins, Ken Doll and Wannabe Ken. Ouch! Much as I tried, I couldn't forget those nicknames. Sandra's must have been less memorable. At least I hoped it was. I wondered which Ken she had married.

"Cassandra's done well for herself. After her parents' accident, she picked herself up and used those God-given powers to launch a successful career. Married as well but no children yet."

God-given powers? While I had enjoyed teaching Sandra, who was polite and well-behaved, I saw no evidence of powers. Only a discipline and determination fostered by old-fashioned immigrant parents who instilled a strong work ethic in their youngest child. They had been much older than Sandra, closer to my parents' age, and a bit harsh at times. I had done my best to smooth the waters and achieved some success. They did allow Sandra to go on a day trip to Martyrs' Shrine in Midland and attend her graduation party.

"You've got some homework to do," Constable Mulligan said. "There'll be nine of us participating in the séance: You, Cassandra, me, Jake, Adam, Kaitlin, Hannah, Daniel, and Bob."

He rattled off the names so quickly, I didn't have time to write anything down. Nor did he provide surnames. I would need to get my hands on the yearbook. There was one somewhere in a box in my storage area, which was closed for the evening. Ten fifteen. Much too late to bother the superintendent in my condo building. I contemplated asking the constable to repeat the names and provide surnames but didn't want to prolong the conversation. "I'll see you tomorrow, Constable Mulligan."

"Uh…it's Leo," he said, as he hung up the telephone.

Leo the Hunk. Another blast from the past.

Chapter 2

Leo the Hunk. Never in a million years did I think I'd hear from him again. After a disastrous blind date that one of the teachers pressured me into accepting, I swore I'd have nothing to do with Leo ever again. I took extra care to avoid streets near the Ontario Provincial Police station, and I turned down invitations to the sports bar he frequented. Nothing against that particular bar. I did like their bison burgers, but I didn't want to run the risk of seeing Leo or recalling the details of the date.

Four hours. Four painful hours where I had to listen to play-by-plays of Leo's glory days as a basketball and hockey star. About how he almost got picked to be a Boston Bruin. And pointed questions about why I wasn't interested in sports and other outdoor activities. It seemed his entire social life revolved around hockey and baseball games with his buds, snowmobiling and skiing during the winters, swimming and water-skiing during the summers. When I didn't ooh and aah over his attractiveness—he had the brooding James Dean look down to perfection—or his athletic prowess, he became snarky.

In the end, we decided that being recently divorced was the only thing we had in common. He did stop talking long enough to hear about Luigi's betrayal. I also listened to the details of his breakup. Leo had fallen head-over-heels in love with a beautiful Torontonian who accepted his marriage proposal and moved to Parry Sound. After two years of living in the small town, she issued an ultimatum—relocate to Toronto or say goodbye to this marriage.

Our respective matchmakers heard all about the disastrous evening, and thankfully no other blind dates were suggested while I lived in Parry Sound.

Ten thirty. I was itching to find out more about Cassandra Coburn. One former student who would have many Google pages. But I had one other task ahead of me. I had to phone my present hunk, who also happened to be a police officer.

Chief Detective Carlo Fantin. My high school crush and current squeeze. In three weeks' time, we would celebrate the second-year anniversary of our reconnection. Right now, he was over two thousand miles away from Sudbury, helping his daughter relocate to Vancouver. We talked every night, sometimes we would even Skype. Not my favorite mode of communication. I was a neophyte when it comes to technology and not too thrilled with having every blemish and wrinkle magnified. I preferred telephone calls or Skype with the auditory-only feature.

To be truthful, I was getting tired of hearing Carlo extol the virtues on living on the West Coast: warmer temperatures, walks along the waterfront, and proximity to his daughter and adorable grandsons. He was also a short plane ride away from his son Steve in Alberta. Each evening, he shared a new reason for leaving Ontario and heading out west. A year away from retirement, he was contemplating all the possibilities ahead. While I also liked the West Coast, I was not ready to leave my eighty-year-old mother alone in Sudbury or pass my two-year-old ReCareering business on to someone else. At least, not on a permanent basis.

I took a deep breath and dialed Carlo's number. He answered on the fourth ring. "Hi, Gilda. I was just about to call." Laughter and voices echoed in the background.

"Are you having a party?"

"It's our last weekend with Steve, Debbie, and the kids. They're leaving Sunday morning for Calgary. We've decided to spend tomorrow on Vancouver Island. The kids had so much fun there last week." I could hear the smile in his voice. "It's the first time all nine of us have been together out here. That hasn't happened often enough."

Steve and Debbie had three children under the age of ten so they couldn't make too many trips out east. But a ninety-minute plane ride to Vancouver was manageable and more affordable. That would be a common occurrence if Carlo decided to move out west after retiring from the police force.

"The kids are so excited. All five of them have been running around the place. I think they'll be ready for bed very soon. And they'll sleep the night." He paused. "How's everything with you?"

For a fraction of a second, I debated saying nothing about Sarah McHenry and tomorrow's séance. But I had learned the hard way that keeping things from Carlo was not a good idea. Last year, he implemented a three-month separation when he felt we weren't communicating. Personally, I believed it had more to do with the arrival of his daughter Tania. Fresh with the wounds of her divorce, she packed up her children, hopped on a plane, and moved to Sudbury.

Tania and I got off to a rocky start, but later managed to reconnect, thanks to the efforts of my mother and godmother. Tania was grateful for the shared meals and offers of free babysitting. Her own mother and grandparents were no longer with us.

I breathed many sighs of relief when her attorney recommended she move back to British Columbia. While her ex-husband didn't want full custody, he did want regular access to the children. Only then would he relinquish their two-thousand-square-foot home and move to a smaller condo in the downtown.

"Gilda! Are you still there?" I could hear the annoyance in Carlo's voice.

"Yes, sorry. I...um...I..." I told him all about Sarah and Leo's call.

"What an ass!" Carlo exploded. "Mulligan shouldn't be asking you or anyone else to help with a murder investigation. Especially a botched-up one. He's got his nerve blaming you for overlooking the email. The woman's been dead three weeks, and he's investigating calls now?" He swore under his breath and added, "He must be new and still undergoing training. An experienced OPP officer would not be so negligent."

Before hooking up with Carlo, I knew very little about the extent of the provincial police's authority in the Ontario. In addition to providing service to rural communities that didn't have their own municipal police forces, these officers patrolled all provincial highways and waterways, investigated province-wide and cross-jurisdictional major crimes, provided protection to visiting politicians and dignitaries, and aided local police whenever the need arose. Carlo and his colleagues spoke highly—sometimes even reverently—of the OPP.

"Sarah had a habit of leaving her cell phone behind," I explained, feeling the need to defend Leo. I still struggled with the server's carelessness. Had I picked up a friend's cell phone, I'd contact her right away. And if she didn't respond, I would alert someone else. Sarah's death should have triggered the server's memory.

"I've got a good mind to call up Mulligan and let him have it." Anger and frustration seeped into Carlo's voice. "Or better still, report him. He needs to have his knuckles rapped."

Exactly what I didn't want to see happen. "It's one night. And I do feel guilty about missing the email."

"Don't. In my experience, when potential victims reach out, it's often too late. What could you have done to prevent her death? Other than urging her to call the local police or call them yourself." He paused. "Maybe she didn't want Mulligan involved."

He had a good point. I would have listened to Sarah and then…well, I don't know. Would I have driven out to Parry Sound? Invited Sarah to visit me in Sudbury? Called her each night? "It's the use of the pronoun 'we' in the email. Others may be in danger. I think that's what Constable Mulligan fears."

"It's Mulligan's job to solve this girl's death. And I don't think the psychic can help. You taught her. What did you think of her powers?"

"She didn't have powers back then." I tried to remember what I had heard from Mel and the other counselors. "She had an accident in her early twenties and almost died. When she woke up from her coma, she had heightened intuitive abilities." I winced as soon as I finished speaking. While I could share this "New Age" talk with friends and colleagues, I knew better than to offer this explanation to Carlo.

Carlo laughed. "I guess it wouldn't hurt to have an entertaining evening. But that's all you contribute to Mulligan's investigation. Stay the night and drive back to Sudbury in the morning."

"Got it." I hadn't planned on spending any more time than necessary in Parry Sound. Seven months of my life had been more than enough.

A crash reverberated through the phone, followed by wails. "Yikes! One of the kids ran into a floor lamp. I've got to go. We're getting back late tomorrow night, so I'll wait until Saturday night before calling." He added. "Remember, one night only."

I bristled at Carlo's final order as a wave of fatigue assaulted me. I glanced at the computer, itching to find out more about Cassandra. But I didn't dare get started with the research. Once on the Internet, I could spend hours researching. I would need to be in top form for tomorrow at work and to be ready for the drive to Parry Sound.

Chapter 3

Friday, October 25, 2013

I tossed and turned all night, imagining all sorts of scenarios, none of them too pleasant. When I finally fell asleep, I dreamt I was back in the Grade Eight classroom and having all sorts of discipline problems. The Barbies strutted around the room while the boys cheered them on. I woke up agitated and when I saw the time—six twenty-five—decided to get up.

I did my yoga stretches and took a longer shower than usual. For breakfast, I had a smoothie, adding half a pint of blueberries for extra brainpower. Two cups of Freedom Fighter coffee and I was ready to face the day. After clearing the dishes, I made my way to the bedroom closet. What does one pack for a psychic-hosted reunion? Tempted to Google the question, I resisted the impulse. At age fifty-three, I didn't need help with wardrobe selection.

I reached the ReCareering office just before eight o'clock. Whenever I arrived this early, I took several minutes to take in the ambiance and appreciate what I had accomplished in less than two years. My thoughts traveled back to the first time I saw this extra-large space. I couldn't believe my good fortune when I followed the real estate agent into the building. The previous tenants had been three accountants, each with their private offices. The space also included a reception area with partitioned sections, a fully-equipped kitchen, two bathrooms, and a utility closet. It had remained vacant for over a year after the accountants retired their practices. No one wanted to pay the exorbitant rent such a space demanded. That is, no one until I came along with my lottery win and the dream of a career counseling practice that catered to boomers.

I was also blessed to have a relative who excelled at interior design. She worked her magic and created the perfect backdrop for ReCareering. She allowed only dusty roses, mint and sea foam greens, and varying shades of ivories. Mint and sea foam greens. I chuckled at the names but could now distinguish between the two shades. For the furniture, she insisted on oak, antique oak to be exact, and had ensured the pieces arrived in time for the grand opening. But the Georgia O'Keeffe prints on the wall were my idea. I loved the feisty artist and hoped her bold prints would inspire my boomer clients to shake up their lives.

When I reached my desk, I scanned my emails and took care of the more pressing ones. I checked the telephone messages. I didn't recognize any of the names, and none of the callers appeared too anxious for my response. I was thankful to Rebecca Trelawny, who handled all queries. I didn't regret my decision to hire her as receptionist, based on two days of temporary work experience. Over the past six months, she had streamlined all our procedures and taken on several bookkeeping tasks as well.

I took out the yearbook I had ferreted out of the storage room. I stroked the familiar burgundy cover, recalling the hundreds of collective hours spent planning and creating the sixty-four-page book. Small by high school standards, but a daunting task for the seventeen eager Grade Eight students who were thrilled to be the first graduating class to have a yearbook.

Throwing out the challenge had calmed down the motley group, as did consistent application of rules and expectations. Grueling days and evenings, but I did turn the class around, and we managed to have the yearbook completed by the end of April and distributed during the last week of June.

I meant to focus on the mug-shot pages, but I couldn't resist rereading the Principal's Message, my message, and that of my co-editors. Sarah McHenry had been a co-editor and Adam Coburn her partner in crime. They made a lovely couple, and I recalled them attending the Grad dance together. Moody Barbie brought out the best in Wannabe Ken, and I suspect Wannabe Ken helped lift her spirits as well. While she did attract considerable male attention, she had to compete with Mean Barbie and Mellow Barbie, who had first pickings. And I suspect that pattern was reinforced throughout Moody Barbie's life.

Sarah McHenry. Sarah McHenry. Sarah McHenry. Adam Coburn. Adam Coburn. Adam Coburn. I needed to put aside those monikers I had worked hard to eradicate.

Two knocks on the door. I glanced up and met Rebecca's surprised glance. "You're here early." She and the other counselors liked to tease me about my banker's hours on Fridays. I liked to come in later, often around nine-thirty or ten. It was one of the many small rebellions against the regimentation of my teaching years. I was determined not to be governed by bells and other constraints. As the boss, I didn't have to answer to anyone. By the same token, I didn't push Rebecca, Belinda, or Mel too hard either. If they needed more flexible hours or time off, I didn't hesitate to give my approval.

I had forgotten about Rebecca's request to leave early. She often volunteered to give her adult children a break and babysit on weekends. This afternoon, she would pick up her five grandchildren—aged four to ten—and take them home for a "Weekend with Grandma."

"You didn't have to come in early." In spite of my assurances that she didn't have to make up the missed time, Rebecca insisted on what she liked to call "balancing the books."

"I'm up anyway. May as well be productive." Rebecca nodded toward the yearbook. "Are you planning to connect with former students?"

If only I could turn back the hands of time, read that email, and connect with Sarah. My throat constricted, and I couldn't speak. I blinked hard, trying hard to keep tears from starting.

"What's wrong, Gilda?" Rebecca sat in the chair across from me and took my hand.

Tears streamed down my cheeks. I hadn't cried when Leo informed me of Sarah's death. Nor had I cried during or after my conversation with Carlo. Rebecca's calm and matter-of-fact demeanor broke through my resistance. I helped myself to several tissues.

Rebecca waited patiently for my tears to subside. To my surprise, I found myself sharing last evening's conversations. All the while, Rebecca's face remained impassive. "Safe and secure as a bank vault," Mel and Belinda often commented. "She's like Switzerland." A neutral, non-judgmental ear—and that's what I needed right now.

As soon as I finished speaking, Rebecca nodded slowly. "Going to Parry Sound is the right thing to do. But I don't think the constable should have played on your guilt. I doubt you could have saved that lost soul." She sighed. "I don't think one séance is going to accomplish too much."

Carlo had hinted at the same thing. I imagine he and Rebecca were on the same page when it came to psychics and other holistic phenomena.

Rebecca sat up straighter. "We have some time before the others arrive. I can be another set of eyes while you look through the yearbook." She winked. "I planned to start the month's end report, but it can wait."

Fridays were our slowest day of the week. Mel, Belinda, and I used those days to finalize client files and get caught up on the week's paperwork. Rebecca used the day to work ahead. No wonder she had accomplished so much in six months!

Rebecca moved her chair next to mine.

I turned to the mug shot pages in the yearbook and located Sarah McHenry. After examining the girl's features, Rebecca pointed to Kaitlin Fraser and Hannah Biltmore. "Those are the other two Barbies?"

I nodded and waited while Rebecca examined each girl closely.

"If I didn't know any better, I'd think they were sisters or cousins."

Long, blonde hair split in the middle and pale

white faces unadorned by makeup. The similarities ended with their hair. Hannah flashed a perfect set of teeth; Kaitlin smiled without opening her mouth; and Sarah pouted.

My gaze gravitated toward Sandra Maddalone's picture. What a sweetheart! Dark hair and eyes framed by Brooke Shields' eyebrows. How she hated those brows and longed to pluck. I had to admit she was one of my pets, and I had a special fondness for her. While I did try to keep it hidden, I knew several of the others—Jake, in particular—suspected the favoritism. But he never said anything. He would smile, shake his head, and wink at me. He had a soft spot for Sandra, but I don't think he acted upon it. They all knew about Sandra's strict Italian parents.

Rebecca followed my glance and chuckled. "I bet she was one of your favorites."

Was I that transparent? Hopefully, none of the other students had picked up on my fondness for Sandra aka Cassandra Coburn.

Rebecca pointed to the laptop on the desk. "Let's start with Cassandra. She'd have the best online platform."

I put the yearbook aside and Googled *Cassandra Coburn Psychic*, and sure enough, millions of hits appeared. I found her website and visited it. When I clicked on her About page, I was greeted by an older, polished Sandra—no, I needed to think of her as Cassandra now. She had changed her name for a reason.

When I decided to take back my maiden name, I didn't face too many problems in southern Ontario. But it took years before friends and former colleagues in

Sudbury stopped addressing me as Gilda Battista.

The bio glossed over the accident that had ended the lives of the elder Maddalones and left Cassandra in a coma for twenty-four days. Had she been alone? I recalled an older brother, Lorenzo, who lived in Kingston, and an aunt, her mother's younger sister, who also lived in Parry Sound. Vera Lodestro would have stepped in and helped Cassandra. Another kind and generous Italian woman who welcomed and often treated me to a home-cooked dinner. I hadn't seen her in years. Was she still alive? I wished I'd kept up our correspondence.

"No pictures of her family," Rebecca said, nodding in approval. "She's smart to keep her website professional and focus on the services offered."

I clicked on her Workshops and Seminars and scrolled through the list. Several titles caught my attention: "How to Manifest Your Goals"; "Heal Thy Self"; "What Happens When We Die?"

More voices and two faces at the door. Mel Nelson and Belinda Rossi. I was so fortunate to have these young women and Rebecca working with me, and I felt confident leaving ReCareering in their very capable hands. But not for too long. Barely out of its infant stage—we would celebrate our second anniversary on Halloween—I wanted to be at the helm for much longer. Not twenty years but at least five more years. And then, well then, I would see what the spirit moved me to do. One of the many perks of a lottery win: I wasn't imprisoned by my circumstances.

"She may be leaving early," Rebecca whispered, loud enough for me to hear.

Mel and Belinda laughed and shook their heads.

"Figured there was a reason for this burst of morning energy," Mel said.

Mel Nelson had come a long way from the Goth-inspired rebel I had first met two years ago. All but two of the piercings were gone, and the asymmetrical ebony cut had been replaced by a warm chestnut pixie. And she had found her calling. After three months of filling in as receptionist, she signed up for the online Career Development Practitioner program and was now two months away from obtaining her diploma. But I hadn't waited before promoting her to career counselor. After only six months, she had a healthy clientele, mainly adolescents and millennials who flocked to the reformed rebel.

Belinda and Mel laughed as they waved and shut the door behind them.

Rebecca glanced at her watch and sighed. "I better get out there." She rose and left the room.

If my two o'clock client canceled—as they often did on Friday afternoons—I would leave early, take in the leaves changing, and maybe stop at the French River Trading Post.

Chapter 4

I minimized Cassandra's website and Googled
Sarah McHenry. As I waited, I took several deep
breaths, knowing what would turn up. And sure
enough, Sarah's obituary was at the top of the first page
of links. I clicked and read:

*The family announces the sudden passing of Sarah
Ann McHenry on Monday, September 30, 2013, at the
age of 35. Beloved daughter of Ann and Stuart
McHenry. Loving sister of Eileen (John Nowicki) of
Hamilton and Conor (Teresa Bartley) of Lethbridge.
Dear aunt of Laura, Jordan, Rachel, and Gloria.
Beloved granddaughter of Catherine McHenry. She will
be sadly missed by her aunts, uncles, cousins and
friends. Sarah's family will receive relatives and friends
from 2-4 and 7-9 on Monday, October 7, 2013. A
private service will be held in the Torrance Chapel on
Tuesday, October 8, 2013, at 11:00 a.m., followed by
burial. As expressions of sympathy, donations to My
Friend's House would be appreciated by the family.
Arrangements entrusted to Torrance Funeral Home &
Chapel in Parry Sound.*

Three weeks ago, Sarah was still alive. Was she
happy with her life choices? I imagined she would have
entered into several relationships during her short life.
Had any of those relationships fulfilled her? What of
her career choices? Leo had said nothing about the

young woman's adult life. Nor had I asked. I was too shell-shocked with the announcement of her death to wonder how she spent the twenty-one years since Grade Eight Graduation.

One thing concerned me, and perhaps it was a moot point. I wondered about the family's decision to accept donations for My Friend's House, a haven for abused women and their children in the Parry Sound area. Was it a random choice? One of Mrs. McHenry's volunteer organizations? Or had the home helped Sarah or her sister?

I also wondered about the absence of a picture. Most obituaries feature either a recent photo or one from the past. At age thirty-five, Sarah would still have the bloom of youth, and I imagine there would be many pictures from which to choose. More references to the obituary filled the first Google page. Moving on to the second and third pages, I found no other details about the Sarah McHenry I once knew, but I did find several variations of the article Leo had sent. I clicked and read several accounts but didn't discover any new information.

The telephone rang, startling me out of my thoughts. My heart beat faster when I saw "unknown number" flash. While I shouldn't be alarmed, I couldn't help but recall the many calls I had fielded six months earlier during the last murder investigation. I picked up after the fifth ring.

"Hi, Gilda. I hope I'm not interrupting. It's Cassandra...uh...Sandra Maddalone." She managed a laugh, a hesitant one. "When I heard you had agreed to come tonight, I asked Leo for your contact information. He gave me this number; I hope you don't mind. I'm calling to invite you for fish and chips tonight." She paused. "Healthy fish and chips."

Fish and chips on the first Friday of the month. A tradition I had shared with the Maddalone family for the seven months I lived in Parry Sound. I didn't know how it started, but it became one of the highlights of my stay in the community. I looked forward to those crisply fried fish fillets and hand-cut fries that tasted oh so good but exceeded my fat and cholesterol quotas for the week. "It's wonderful to hear from you, Sandra. I'd love to come for dinner. But just how healthy are you making them?"

She laughed, and I joined in. While we loved our mothers' cooking, we had to abandon many of their methods, especially those involving deep frying.

"I'm also including dessert." She paused. "It'll be just the two of us. Jake is having a boy's night out with his son, Dougie. He'll be back in time for the séance."

She married the Ken Doll. I would have thought her more suited to Adam, the less flamboyant twin, but that was before her amazing transformation. I was happy to hear it would be dinner for two. "I'm looking forward to catching up and learning more about Sarah's life."

"We'll catch up first. Sarah...well I don't know how to put this kindly. I would describe her as a cautionary tale." Cassandra paused. "I don't want to dwell on her too much before the séance. I need to have a clean mental slate beforehand."

A cautionary tale. If I had more time, I would pursue the topic now. But only ten minutes remained before the arrival of my first client of the day. "Yes, we have so much to talk about. I'll be there around five."

"Perfect!" She gave me her address and hung up.

Dougie. Dougie Coburn. Could that be short for Douglas? If memory served me correctly, Jake's father was named Douglas. Cassandra had referred to Dougie as Jake's son, suggesting a previous marriage or relationship. Not too surprising, considering Jake's good looks and charm. I would learn more later today.

Chapter 5

Beatrice Sartor had started coming in every Friday since the beginning of September. With her children in high school, Beatrice found herself at loose ends. After making breakfast and seeing them off, she had too many hours of unstructured time ahead of her. She spent most of her time finishing up sewing projects and cooking gourmet meals no one appreciated. And still, there was too much time left over.

Her husband often worked late and would pick up fast food or meet his friends at the pub before coming home. As for her daughters, they lamented the changes in cuisine and fiddled with the food on their plates. Beatrice was convinced one of them was anorexic and the other two simply difficult. Beatrice needed to do something for herself, and she figured she might as well earn money doing it. Joining the gym or a volunteer organization held no appeal, at least not at this point in her life. "I want to work while I still have time to build up a nice nest-egg and contribute to a pension." While she never mentioned her age, I suspected she was somewhere between forty-five and fifty-five.

A worthy goal, but one that would take planning and patience. She grudgingly agreed to the timeline I suggested and had completed all her tasks to date. I had administered several Interest Inventories and coaxed her into role-playing exercises. She needed to be in control. Having ruled the home roost for almost twenty years, she wanted a leadership position.

Unfortunately, she was not ready to enter the workplace. Her business diploma and five years' experience as teller and loan officer looked good on paper, but she had not updated her skills since leaving the workplace after the birth of her first child sixteen years ago. She balked at the thought of taking more courses. "I'm too old, and I don't want to sit in a class with students who could be my children. I deal with enough drama at home."

During our first session, I made the mistake of asking her to elaborate and had to listen to forty-five minutes of teenage angst and rebellion. Thankfully, our subsequent sessions ran more smoothly, and she responded well to all my instructions. She researched several retail businesses and was prepared to work as a sales associate at a ladies shop. A stepping stone to the managerial career that would suit her take-charge personality.

Today, she appeared trim and happy in her pink tweed suit and black blouse. A tall woman with short brown hair and expressive brown eyes, she reminded me of a younger Joan Collins. Something was up. While she had dressed well for each session, she appeared more tailored and polished today.

"We'll have to cut this appointment short." She waved a folder and beamed at me. "I've got an interview in one hour's time."

"Where?" I must admit I was surprised. We had finalized her cover letter and résumé last week. And from what I could recall, she had sent out only two queries.

"Northern Reflections in the Southridge Mall." She paused. "If it had been the New Sudbury branch, I would have canceled this session."

Northern Reflections stores had been around for over three decades. A trusted Canadian brand, the stores offered fashionable and comfortable women's clothing. Most of the sales associates were fashion-conscious women over forty. A good fit for Beatrice. We spent the next thirty minutes reviewing possible interview questions. I have to admit, she performed well. In spite of her grumbling, she had listened and visited all the information sites I recommended. Barring some unforeseen event, she would get the job, and I could see her moving up the career ladder. I wished her well and returned to my sleuthing.

Knowing Sandra was married to Jake, I now had someone else to investigate. *Cassandra. Cassandra.* I needed to address her as Cassandra, not Sandra or Sandy. She had changed her name for a reason, and I had to honor the change. When I took back my maiden name, I wasn't thrilled when long-time friends and relatives introduced me as Gilda Battista. It took almost two years to get everyone on board with my name change. Sometimes, I would get junk mail addressed to G. Battista, and, of course, the infamous email I had missed. Had Sarah addressed me as Gilda Greco, I might not have filed it away. Or maybe I needed to figure out why the mention of Luigi Battista's name still triggered me.

I Googled Jake Coburn and got over four hundred and fifty thousand hits. I clicked on Google Images and located him halfway down the page. Time and genetics had favored him. With his thick mop of sandy brown hair and sky blue eyes, he was rocking the boy-next-door look. Or should I say man-next-door? I could imagine him spending his summer weekends sailing on Georgian Bay or golfing at one of the many courses in the area, and during the winter participating in all the winter sports the North had to offer.

A few more clicks revealed his profession. An unlikely choice, based on what I recalled of the high-energy, mischievous adolescent I had once taught. Jake had pursued an accounting career and joined his father at Coburn & Peterson Accountants. When I tried to access his Facebook account, I found it set to privacy. A wise choice considering the trajectory of Cassandra's career.

Cassandra Coburn's Facebook page was all about her psychic business. She had thousands of friends, and most of her comments referred to specific events. She also shared quotations, provided links to motivational and inspirational sites, and sent good wishes to visitors. But nothing hinting at a personal or family life.

I noted the glowing praise and appreciation in the visitor comments:

"You saved my life."
"You're the goddess."
"I can function now."
"You're the real thing."

Adam Coburn was next on my list. Again lots of possibilities but none of the Google images came close. While he didn't have Jake's drop-dead-gorgeous looks, he had a quiet charm that I and many others found endearing. The girls lusted after Jake but confided in Adam. I often thought he would make an excellent therapist or even minister. But I hadn't voiced those sentiments to anyone, and in particular not to his mother, who wouldn't have accepted any suggestions regarding her sons.

A tall woman, Margaret Coburn stood well over six feet with her high heels and towered over her husband, a quiet man who said very little at parent-teacher interviews. Margaret kept her hair in a chestnut brown chin-length bob, and no matter the time of day or the weather, it appeared perfect. I never saw one hair out of place, and sometimes I'd stare at her head and try to figure out how she did it.

She made no secret that Jake was her favorite and would spend most of the interview chatting about all his future prospects. Whenever I brought up his rambunctious behavior and tendency to do as he pleased, she waved her hand. "Boys will be boys," was her motto. As for Adam, she would smile tightly and shake her head. She had little respect for his more artistic temperament and barely acknowledged his position as co-editor of the yearbook.

I moved on to Hannah Biltmore aka Mellow Barbie. Had she remained mellow or toughened up? Again, too many possibilities, and I counted five blondes who could be Hannah on the Google Images site. The same for Kaitlin Fraser aka Mean Barbie. Cassandra had taken on Jake's surname, and perhaps the other two girls had followed suit.

Who was left? I racked my brain for the two remaining students, but nothing came to mind. I hadn't copied down their names, and Carlo's call had rattled me. I would find out more when I met with Cassandra.

The rest of the morning dragged. Two 30-something men with back-to-back appointments depleted my energy and patience. I'm usually more willing to listen to their angst, but today I had seventeen former students in my mind, one of whom was no longer with us. I wanted to shake some sense into the two millennials who were whining about the evil day jobs that were sucking their creativity and joie de vivre.

When I conceived the idea of ReCareering, my intention had been to help other boomers transition into second careers or retirement. But according to Mel's statistics for the previous year, over eighty percent of our clients were under the age of forty. Less than five percent were over fifty-five.

As soon as the second millennial left, I buzzed Rebecca and asked her not to disturb me for the next thirty minutes. While most of our walk-ins came on Mondays and Tuesdays, I didn't want to deal with another disgruntled millennial.

I made my way to the small kitchenette and retrieved my plastic container from the fridge. Tofu Cacciatore. Whenever Carlo was away, I would experiment with different tofu recipes. And there would usually be leftovers. This was one of my favorites, and I could eat it every day. Even my mother approved of what she had first referred to as the bastardization of an Italian classic—chicken cacciatore. One o'clock was later than usual. Hopefully, the protein-laden meal would tide me over until dinner time.

Chapter 6

My two o'clock client was early and well-prepared for our session. Another middle-aged woman who did her homework, but she was less emotional than Beatrice and more open to entry-level positions. I didn't have the patience for any more drama or whining. Not the best attitude for a career counselor, but the previous night's revelations had put me on edge. I was itching to get on the road and help solve Sarah's senseless death and prevent another tragedy. The appointment flew and by ten after three I was in my car. I filled up with gas and stopped to buy a bottle of wine for Cassandra.

As I passed the city limits, I felt myself relaxing. I inserted Adele's latest CD and let the music fill the car. I kept my windows down and breathed in the crisp, autumn air. While the long and winding road could be challenging during the winter months, I thoroughly enjoyed my drive during the other seasons, especially autumn, when I could feast on the riotous beauty of color that Mother Nature bestowed upon those of us living in the Northern Hemisphere. It took less than ninety minutes to reach Parry Sound.

My heart quickened as I took the exit into the town. The first time I had followed this particular route was two weeks after Luigi had ended our year-long marriage. Well, not exactly one year. Technically speaking, our marriage lasted one year less a day. And I was partly to blame. I should have picked up on all those troublesome signs during our two dating years and six-month engagement.

But at age twenty-nine, I had too many bridesmaid dresses in my closet and was tired of waiting for Mr. Right, so I decided to settle for Mr. Right Now. Luigi and I taught at the same high school in Sudbury. We were both introverts and loved to spend our leisure time reading, going to theater and movies, hiking, snowshoeing, and cross-country skiing. A perfect match—at least that's what my parents, relatives, and friends thought. In my mind, I added "almost" to the perfect match, realizing I would have to work at the relationship. I hadn't realized how hard.

Luigi had also felt the pressure to marry but thought he could have his cake and eat it, too. He married but continued to seek the attention of other men. One man in particular, Claude Noel de Tilly, wanted a more exclusive relationship, and Luigi gave it to him.

My state of mind had been a very fragile one. I recalled crying and stopping several times along the highway to compose myself. At one point, I even considered returning to Sudbury and moving back into my parents' house. A safe and easy—too easy—solution that would have been disastrous. I would have continued to retreat into myself and never moved beyond Luigi's betrayal.

After a quick stop at the Comfort Inn, I set out for Cassandra's house. With the help of my GPS, I arrived twenty minutes early.

Tidy and unpretentious, the split-level brick house reminded me of the Maddalone home in which

Cassandra was raised. For some reason, I had expected a nationally-known psychic to live in a more upscale home with large acreage. I also wondered about Jake's preferences. Having been raised in a stately colonial where Margaret Coburn ensured every detail met her exacting standards, Jake would either want to continue living that way or perhaps rebel against all the pretentiousness and live more simply.

As I raised my hand to ring the doorbell, the front door opened, and I was engulfed in a tight hug. When we separated, I took a long look at Cassandra. "*Bellissima*!" I whispered. Even without a trace of makeup and with her hair brushed back, she was stunning. And she was so slim, at least three sizes smaller than during her adolescent days.

"Ditto!" she said as she smiled and nodded. "Back then, I could see the inner beauty even though you tried to disguise it with hardly any makeup and old lady clothes. And now, well now, your outer beauty matches your inner glow." She closed her eyes and held out her hands. "And you are in love with someone who is worthy of you."

I shivered. I wasn't ready for her powers. Or hocus-pocus as Carlo called it. But I had to be careful not to judge Cassandra. From what I had read this morning, she had built a very successful career as a psychic. And Leo Mulligan—who didn't have an airy-fairy bone in his body—believed in her powers. I punched her arm. "What do you mean by old lady clothes? And what can you tell me about Carlo?"

She eyed me critically. "You wore those long skirts and shapeless tops that hid your slender frame." She waved her hand toward the kitchen. "I'll tell you all about my gifts later, but first come in and let's get settled."

I followed Cassandra into the living room, beautifully decorated in an ice-cream palette. A large Buddha artwork hung over the fireplace and bookcases dominated two of the walls. We ended up in the kitchen, where the round table had been set with placemats and cutlery. A tray with lightly breaded fish and another with fries lay on the counter. A bowl with a spinach salad was also on the counter.

"I hope you don't mind sitting here." She shrugged. "With you, it feels more comfortable chatting in a kitchen. It reminds me of—uh..." She faltered and blinked back tears.

I leaned over and squeezed her arm. "It's okay, Cassandra. We don't have to talk about your parents." Signora Matilda and Signor Giorgio. From the start, I had used the honorary titles, a habit my mother had insisted upon when addressing older people. Signora Matilda had mildly protested, but I could tell she approved. As for Signor Giorgo, he went along with whatever his wife deemed acceptable.

"But I want to tell you." She swallowed hard. "I have to tell someone about...well...the accident and..." She got up and turned her back on me as she turned on the oven heat.

I heard myself gasp. An involuntary sound I'm certain she heard as well. "Didn't you talk to someone afterward?" Anyone who had survived a serious accident and spent weeks in a coma would need counseling. And it wouldn't be limited to a handful of sessions. Post-traumatic stress was a real risk, and, in this case, Cassandra would have needed help with survivor guilt and adjusting to her raised levels of intuitiveness.

"I saw three different therapists and then I found my own spiritual advisor later." A wide smile erupted. "Priscilla helped with my psychic practice, but she doesn't get the Italian stuff. You know…how my parents were…and what they expected."

I nodded. Her parents were much older than her schoolmates' parents and could have been my parents. Had they lived in Sudbury or any city with a sizeable Italian population, they would have connected with their countrymen and modified their parenting styles. Seeing other Italians adapt to North American traditions might have nudged them to give Cassandra more freedom. Also, there would have been more opportunities for Cassandra to socialize and commiserate with Italian girls in her age group. Only a handful of Italians lived in Parry Sound and most of them were northern Italians.

One southern Italian family was related to the Maddalones. Vera Lodestro was Cassandra's maternal aunt. While Vera was a decade younger than Mrs. Maddalone and less rigid, she had her hands full with her own five children and a live-in mother-in-law. Also, Vera hadn't yet had the experience of adolescence and its challenges.

During the seven months I lived in Parry Sound, I did intercede on Cassandra's behalf several times, and her parents appeared to soften their stances. But high school would have presented more issues and conflicts.

Cassandra poured two large glasses of wine and placed a cheese and fruit platter on the table. We clinked glasses and sipped our wine. While I longed to hear about Sarah, I knew I couldn't initiate that conversation without upsetting Cassandra. In any event, I was more than curious to hear Cassandra's story. "I want to hear all the details, everything that happened after I left Parry Sound."

Cassandra put down her glass and leaned over to hug me. "I'm so glad you've come. I...all of us...we need your help."

We need your help. Goosebumps rose on my arms. What on earth was she talking about? And what had been going on with my former students that suddenly needed my attention?

Chapter 7

Cassandra stared beyond me, at a fixed point somewhere in space. While I hadn't interacted with too many psychics, I knew she had moved to another plane, possibly a spiritual one. I leaned back and made myself comfortable, ready to listen as she shared her story.

"High school wasn't as bad as I thought it would be. After you left, Aunt Vera got more involved in my life. I don't know if you spoke to her, or if she realized that constant intervention was needed if I was to survive and thrive in my parents' house. For the most part, my parents listened to her and did give me more freedom. But I never felt comfortable inviting too many friends to the house, other than Yvonne Dupuis and Cathy Martin."

Big Mouse and Little Mouse. I couldn't believe their nicknames came to mind so quickly. Such is the power of those early monikers. Even after two decades, I could still associate those dreaded nicknames with the students. While perusing the yearbook, I recalled most of the nicknames but not Cassandra's. I imagine the students also had instantaneous recall, and I wouldn't be too surprised if the nicknames still crept up whenever they met.

"I dated two boys I met in high school, but nothing too serious. I didn't want to start any relationship that could trigger conversations of engagements and weddings. One thing my parents both agreed upon was higher education for both sexes." She paused and made a face. "But it had to be what they thought was practical; in my case, a business degree. And it had to be at Laurentian University in Sudbury. They wouldn't hear of me going any further. After Lorenzo abdicated his responsibilities, I was left to run Maddalone Cleaning Services. They weren't prepared to hand the fruits of all their hard work to a stranger."

With two elementary school educations between them, the Maddalones had managed to start and build a successful cleaning business. But that hadn't been their first goal. Signor Giorgio would have preferred to settle in the Niagara Peninsula and buy a farm or winery, but aging parents in Sudbury and Signora Matilda's resistance to the rural lifestyle derailed his plans. After six months of working in the nickel mines, Signor Giorgio called it quits and moved to Parry Sound, leaving behind his startled parents. But always the dutiful son, he did visit every other Sunday for the rest of their lives.

In the early days, they worked for cash, under the table, and too often they were treated like they belonged under the table. Their horror stories made my blood run cold: Customers would take last-minute vacations and forego housecleaning service for a couple of weeks, not paying them. Some clients complained about the cost and often added extra duties with very little notice or offering to pay extra. "I'm way behind on the laundry, can you pitch in?"; "It's time for window washing"; "I've got my granddaughter for the day. Would you mind looking in on her while you clean? I've got lots of errands to run."

I turned my attention back to Cassandra, who was busy putting trays of food in the oven. She set the timer and sat.

"As soon as I turned sixteen, I helped with the small house-cleaning jobs during the summers and breaks. While I was getting my business degree, I started spending more time with the bookkeeper. They were grooming me to take over, just like they had done with Lorenzo before he married the Rabbit."

To this day, any mention of rabbits conjures up visions of the younger Mrs. Maddalone, who lured Lorenzo and derailed all future plans. Lorenzo, who was twelve years older than Cassandra, was also expected to obtain a business degree. But some survival instinct must have existed within him. Instead of attending Laurentian University, he chose Queens in Kingston, a good three hundred miles away, much too far for weekly or even monthly visits home.

During his third month on campus, he met Silvana Lisi, a pretty and petite library assistant who was five years older and itching to get married. They connected and became an item. Still living at home, Silvana, with her parents' help, wined and dined the lonely young man from northern Ontario. At the end of his first year in Kingston, Lorenzo moved into the upstairs apartment of Silvana's aunt, who happened to live on the same street.

Lorenzo's trips home became fewer and fewer. During the summer, he found work with a construction company that paid much more than the cleaning business. By the end of his second year, Lorenzo and Silvana were engaged. Unable to wait, they married during Christmas of that year. Within nine months,

Silvana had her first child and proceeded to get pregnant two more times within the next four years.

At age twenty-five, Lorenzo had a wife, three children under the age of five, two jobs, and a hefty mortgage on a two-thousand-square-foot home in Kingston. Visits to Sudbury were out of the question. And whenever the elder Maddalones visited, they were greeted with never-ending chores in a noisy, erratic household where no one could sleep for more than a handful of hours. The Maddalones cursed the daughter-in-law who had foiled all their well-laid plans and inadvertently derailed any plans Cassandra would have had.

I donned my career counselor hat. "What would you have liked to do?"

Cassandra shrugged. "I did well in all my high school courses and would have loved to experiment and take philosophy, psychology, and anthropology courses. Maybe dabble in a third language. But all that uncertainty wouldn't fly, at least not in my parents' house. As far as they were concerned, you went to university to get a good job or improve your earning power."

She was still young enough to go back to school and get a different kind of degree. But I suspect she didn't want to resurrect a vague dream from her adolescent years. In spite of all that happened, a business degree had probably served her well in her psychic business.

Cassandra took a long sip of wine and lowered her eyes. "On Graduation Day, we were coming back from Sudbury. It was one of those perfect June days, not a cloud in the sky and balmy weather. Probably close to seventy degrees and not a trace of humidity. With a light shift underneath, I had not felt too warm in my gown. As soon as the ceremony was over, we hopped in the car, and I took the wheel without asking. I had noticed my father dozing off during the long ceremony, and I didn't want to chance any accidents on the road." She swallowed hard and closed her eyes.

I squeezed her hand as grief and guilt, and most likely remorse flitted across Cassandra's face. Emotions that every surviving driver of a horrific accident must feel for months, maybe even years longer. Did those disquieting feelings ever leave them?

Cassandra continued, "Halfway home, my mother started complaining to my father. They sat in the back seat and whispered. I caught fragments—'…too long…my legs feel like dead weights'…'I can hardly wait to get home.' But I heard her last comment loud and clear. 'If only today we had been attending Sandra's wedding.'

"I turned around to respond, to tell her that her comment was hurtful and inappropriate on a day when they should be celebrating one of my greatest achievements. But as I did, Papa cried out, 'Sandra! You're missing the turn.' I looked back at the road to see the turn, but as I did, I hit the accelerator by mistake, and the car surged forward. And then there was blackness until I woke up twenty-four days later."

Tears streamed down Cassandra's face as she broke off into a loud sob. I moved over and held her close. So many emotions swirled in my own mind. How could her mother be so cruel and thoughtless on her daughter's graduation day? And what did she expect after micro-managing Cassandra's social life for so long? But I couldn't lambast her parents. Instead, I had to deal with the immense guilt Cassandra was experiencing. Senseless and unnecessary guilt that needed to be eradicated if Cassandra were to move on with her life. She had been carrying this load for too long.

I continued to stroke her hair as she cried. "You have nothing to feel guilty about here. And I don't think your parents would want you to feel guilty either." I took several breaths. "Your parents had elementary educations. The concept of rigorous study for four years and getting a degree didn't resonate with their life experiences. While you only heard her last comment, I suspect she might have also said, 'Sandra's beautiful and smart. Why don't these Canadian men snap her up? If she were in Italy, they'd be lining up to ask her out.' "

"They've visited me several times in my sleep." Cassandra managed a smile. "They came last night. I know they approved of you."

In spite of my divorce—still a major scandal in Italian communities during the 1990s—Signora Matilda and Signor Giorgio welcomed me and relaxed whenever I visited. I would have liked to hear more about the nocturnal visits—I suspect many dead people visit psychics in their sleep—but I also wanted to hear about Cassandra's powers. "What happened after you woke up from the coma?"

Cassandra shook her head in amazement. "The doctors were surprised to find nothing wrong with me. While I was weak and disoriented, all my physical and mental faculties were fine. After two weeks, I started to have peculiar symptoms. Whenever I closed my eyes, I could feel myself speeding through total darkness toward a soft light far away. I smelled and heard nothing, and more importantly, I was unafraid. I could still wiggle my fingers and flex my toes, but I had no desire to sit up or stretch my arms and glance in any other direction but straight ahead." She shivered. "I became aware of a warm place inside my chest that was not part of me. It was like…like an unknown presence, knowing and alive, and it conveyed a startling new idea to me. *Use your powers wisely. You can help others improve their lives.* I recall speaking out loud and asking: 'What powers?' And then there would be silence followed by a warm breeze and a soft light encircling me. I could see it through closed eyelids, and I could almost touch it." She paused.

I found her story fascinating and wondered if other psychics had similar stories to share. I had always thought you were born a psychic but perhaps traumatic experiences were needed to awaken or trigger these powers.

Cassandra spoke again. "When I told the doctors, they became concerned and scheduled a battery of CT scans and MRIs. Neurologists were called in from Toronto and Hamilton, but nothing could be found. Lorenzo wanted to call in someone from the States, but I stopped him. I was tired of all the poking around, and by that time, I had begun to feel the stirrings of my heightened intuitiveness."

"How did it manifest itself?" I asked.

"I seemed to know what the doctors would say before they said it." Her mouth compressed into a thin line. "I heard all of Silvana's unspoken concerns. She was afraid I wouldn't recover enough to live on my own. Lorenzo wanted me to move closer to Kingston, but I knew that Silvana didn't approve. I also knew I wouldn't heal if I lived near her. I needed to be around people who loved and nurtured me."

I had never met Silvana, but I had somehow absorbed the elder Maddalones' antipathy toward her. "You must have felt very much alone."

Cassandra shook her head and smiled. "Aunt Vera visited each day. Yvonne's mother came regularly, and so did many of former classmates. Even Meanie."

"Meanie?" And then I remembered Mean Barbie aka Kaitlin Fraser.

Cassandra blushed. "Sorry! I meant Kaitlin."

"It's all right. I'm not your teacher anymore." I chuckled. "I'm surprised those nicknames have lingered for so long."

Cassandra's lips curled into a smile. "Jake came every day."

I raised my eyebrows in surprise. The Jake Coburn I remembered wouldn't have enjoyed spending any more time than necessary in a hospital. He was too fidgety to sit down for more than a few minutes. He was an outdoor boy who would start looking out the window a good fifteen minutes before recess.

"I know. I know. The Ken Doll and hospitals don't go together. But he had another reason for coming each day. His mother was dying. Her ovarian cancer had metastasized, and she was in severe pain. He would visit Mrs. Coburn first and then come to my room. That's when I got to know him, and he got to know me."

Like every other girl in that Grade Eight class, Cassandra had a crush on Jake. While he smiled and joked with all the girls in the class, he focused on the Barbies, with Kaitlin getting the lion's share of his attention.

Cassandra continued. "I don't know how much you know of Jake's story."

"Jake's story?"

"I'm sure you remember how we all went ga-ga over him in class. Well, the Barbies won that particular contest. Kaitlin was his steady for most of the spring. But once the Grad dance was over, she broke it off. She wanted a fresh slate for high school. In high school, Jake played the field for most of the time. In his senior year, he and Hannah started going out together. It was pretty serious, and they ended up at Western after graduation. Hannah got pregnant partway through the year and came back to Parry Sound. Jake was ready to marry her, but Mrs. Coburn wouldn't allow it. She played on his guilt and made him promise not to get married until after he graduated from university." Cassandra paused and bit her lip.

"And then Jake connected with you."

"Never in my wildest dreams did I expect to have anything happen. But we talked and shared. I heard about his hopes for the future and how much he loved and cherished his son Dougie. I got to know the real Jake, not just the handsome stud everyone thought he was." She got a dreamy expression on her face.

I didn't know how long they had been married, but it appeared Cassandra was still on her honeymoon. To be truthful, I hadn't seen much in Jake beyond the superficial. But I had taught them for only seven months, and I hadn't had too many dealings with Jake, other than reprimanding him for flirting and distracting the others.

Cassandra resumed her story. "Mrs. Coburn died while I was still in the hospital. I couldn't attend her funeral." Tears sprang into her eyes. "I couldn't even attend my parents' funerals. Aunt Vera and Lorenzo took care of everything. When I left the hospital, I went back to our house. Aunt Vera had persuaded Lorenzo not to sell until after I had fully recovered. Part of me wanted to stay in my parents' house and mourn, but I soon realized I needed to move on. I was free...free to leave Parry Sound and start over anywhere else. But I didn't want to leave."

"You had a reason to stay."

Cassandra nodded, a sudden stillness coming over her features. "Jake started to talk about us as a couple. I was worried about Hannah's reaction and how she would feel. Dougie was three years old and attached to Jake. Hannah had been waiting for so long but—"

"The heart wants what the heart wants," I said, realizing that I was quoting Luigi's final words to me. It was the only way he could justify leaving me for another man.

"It was hard at first. Hannah wouldn't speak to me, and Kaitlin assumed her full Meanie self. Many of the locals tsked whenever they saw me. But Aunt Vera was in my corner. She confided that my mother would have approved. Mama had often commented about Jake's good looks and his...well...royal connections."

"Royal connections?" I paused and then smiled to myself, recalling Mrs. Coburn's brush with royalty. When Queen Elizabeth visited Ontario in the late 1950s, several people were presented, among them the lovely and accomplished Margaret Coburn, who had been born in England. A picture had been taken and shared in the local newspaper. How did I know about it? When I assigned a family tree project, Jake and Adam had included copies of the photo on their Bristol boards. And, of course, shared the story.

Cassandra laughed. "Mama had hoped I would marry Jake. That is, before Hannah got pregnant." She shivered. "At some level, I felt she had sent Jake to me in atonement for the hurtful comment she had made."

The oven timer rang. Cassandra sprang into action. Within minutes, she plated our food and set the dishes on the table. We said a quick grace and started eating.

Chapter 8

Everything from the light, well-seasoned tilapia to the oven-roasted sweet potato fries to the spinach salad was delicious. I complimented Cassandra several times and asked for the recipes. She smiled and rose to get what looked like a crisp of some kind. I held up my hands in protest, but she shook her head. "It's a peach and blueberry crisp. Hardly any calories at all." She proceeded to cut two generous pieces.

"You are your mother's daughter."

"Thank you," she said, visibly pleased. "I have all her recipes, you know. I've adapted most of them. But the pasta recipes, well, I can't bear to lighten those up. Jake loves them just the way they are."

I nodded in agreement. While I complained about the extra pounds that would creep up after eating one of my mother's signature pasta dishes, I didn't hesitate to accept the invitation whenever she made her calorie-laden lasagna or cannelloni. And Carlo was more than willing to accompany me.

"I feel so much lighter," Cassandra said as she leaned over to squeeze my arm. "Priscilla was right. She said I would feel better once I unloaded all the past angst."

Priscilla? And then I remembered Cassandra's spiritual advisor. I wanted to hear more about the past, but it didn't look like Cassandra wanted to continue with that topic. Her eyes sparkled with delight, and she hummed to herself. When she started to load the dishwasher, I got up to help scrape dishes. As we worked, Cassandra commented on the burst of Indian summer we had been enjoying and her plans for the weekend.

She would be busy both days with the Fall Holistic Fair at the Bobby Orr Community Centre. I was surprised to hear that over eighty psychics and practitioners would be participating. Cassandra would deliver the keynote address on Saturday.

"What time?" I asked. I had missed Cassandra's lecture in Sudbury last fall and would love to hear her speak on "Developing Your Intuitive Abilities."

"Nine thirty. I'll speak for about an hour and then open it up to questions."

"I'll stay." I was in no rush to get home. I had evening plans to see a movie, but the rest of the day was free.

She clapped her hands in delight and started to speak. But the opening of the front door and two male voices stopped her. She lowered her voice. "Adam's back in town, and he's…uh…well he's recovering from another bout of depression."

I had always had a soft spot for Adam and tried hard to bolster his confidence. Being in the same class as a handsome, extroverted sibling was not easy. And it didn't help that his mother favored Jake. Mr. Coburn tried to compensate for his wife's favoritism, but I don't think it was enough to offset the constant battery of criticism and sarcasm. During our after-school yearbook sessions, Adam confided that he never felt smart enough, coordinated enough, or good enough.

Jake walked ahead. I recognized him from his Facebook picture. As soon as he saw me, his smile widened, and he rushed forward to hug me. "Gilda! Is it possible you have de-aged? You look even lovelier than you did twenty years ago."

What a charmer! In spite of myself, I smiled and gave him the once-over. Every hair in place and signs of a summer tan still lingering. His blue eyes sparkled and crinkled a bit, but the final effect was a flattering one. Bradley Cooper came to mind. Jake Coburn would age well, of that I was certain.

I turned my attention to Adam, who was standing behind his brother, waiting patiently for his turn. I tried not to show my shock as I took in the receding hairline and crow's feet that had taken permanent residence around Adam's eyes, still beautiful in color, but there were tinges of sadness and suffering. He also appeared puffier in his face and overall body frame. While Jake could pass for late twenties, I would put Adam's outer age well into the forties. Life had not been kind to Adam Coburn.

I hugged Adam and held him close. I hoped we would have time for a long chat. I wanted to find out more about his past suffering and try to help him. From what Cassandra had said, I gathered Adam had lived elsewhere for a while. A wise move on his part. What had gone wrong? And why had he returned to Parry Sound?

"I'm glad you're here," Adam whispered. "I've wanted to write…but…" He bowed his head. In shame or embarrassment? Whatever had ensued in the past, he could get over it. I would help.

"It's okay. I'm not one for maintaining

correspondence." The last letter I received from Adam had been well over fifteen years ago. He had graduated high school and received several scholarships and bursaries. In the end, he had chosen to pursue an engineering program at the University of Waterloo.

Engineering was a popular choice for students who excelled in mathematics and science, but it often proved disappointing. I couldn't recall too many students who enjoyed the career. Many of them ventured into computer science or went back and pursued an MBA.

Jake laughed. "I think I'm persona non grata here."

I frowned at Jake and took in Cassandra's and Adam's puzzled looks.

Jake pointed to the three of us. "You were her pets. The rest of us...well...we were chopped liver."

I recalled Jake's sly glances and winks. He had those people skills down pat at an early age. But I couldn't resist teasing him. "Now, Jake, you know I treated all of you with the utmost respect."

"But you liked these two the best." He held up his hands. "And I was okay with it. But I didn't like you razzing me all the time."

I shook my finger at him. "Only when you flirted or disrupted—"

"Which was practically all the time," Adam finished. Cassandra nodded in agreement.

Jake raised his arms. "I'm outnumbered here. So, I will concede defeat." He pointed to his watch and raised his eyebrows at Cassandra.

Cassandra turned to me. "I need time to prepare for the séance."

"I need to pick up more wine," Jake said. "I'll leave the two of you to reminisce."

I smiled to myself. Obviously planned beforehand, but I was more than okay with the poorly disguised subterfuge. Glancing at Adam, I could sense him relaxing.

After Cassandra and Jake left, Adam and I made our way to the family room. Another beautiful room but decorated in a more masculine palette. An even larger fireplace with a striking moose head hung over the fireplace. The walls were filled with photographs of different landscapes and seascapes. I wondered who was the photographer—Cassandra or Jake?

"I…I don't know where to start," Adam said as he glanced at his hands.

"How about we begin with where we left off," I said as I leaned back in the cushions. "You were starting your studies at the University of Waterloo."

He winced. "I thought everything would be magical once I left Parry Sound. But it didn't turn out that way at all. I felt like a fish out of water. I began to realize how much I depended upon Jake to break the ice for me. I followed his lead, and, well…got the girls who were willing to settle for Wannabe Ken."

"Stop it!" While I detested the use of those nicknames, I couldn't abide any of them personalizing the monikers.

"No use sugar-coating, Gilda. That's the way it was, and I guess I settled for it. At Waterloo, I realized I'd have to make the first move, but I struggled with approaching girls. I should have steered away from noisy bars and large parties. Stuck with smaller groups and befriended the girls in my classes." He groaned and lowered his head into his hands.

Tempted to offer my favorite platitude from Maya

Angelou—*When you know better, you will do better*—I stroked his arm as I waited for him to continue.

"To give myself more confidence, I started drinking more and...I got into drugs as well. Started with pot and worked up to coke. More coke as I needed it."

Tears stung at my eyes as visions of the lost, troubled young man succumbing to all those temptations came to mind. I had to hold them back as I comforted Adam. Why hadn't he contacted me? I lived a short thirty-minute drive away in Guelph and could have hopped over. But there was no point reminding Adam of what could have been. It would only add to his overwhelming regret.

Adam ran his fingers through his thinning hair and sighed, his face tense. "I blew off the semester and ended up in rehab. When Dad came down to get me, he made it clear I couldn't return to Parry Sound. He and Mom were having marital problems. I found out later that Mom had filed for divorce but recanted when she received her cancer diagnosis in the spring. I don't know the details. Jake knows more, but he's not too forthcoming when it comes to rehashing the past."

Margaret Coburn placed too much importance on appearances and wouldn't have taken such a drastic step without just cause. Thinking back, I could recall very few details about Douglas Coburn. Some of the other teachers often commented about his looks, but other than that, he was considered a definite Yin partner to his wife's overbearing Yang personality.

Adam continued. "I got it together, and U of W took me back. I hunkered down and focused on my studies. I dated but nothing lasted. Usually, the girls ended it." He smiled. "One pretty Italian girl—Teresa—reminded me of you, Gilda. But she wanted to get married as soon as she graduated. When I demurred, she moved on."

Getting that MRS within months of the BA had been the MO in my day. I recalled several of my classmates flashing those large rocks as they waved their diplomas. Graduated in June...married in August...first baby the following June. Thankfully, young women today weren't in any rush to get married. Age thirty was soon enough, with ample time to have one or two babies before thirty-five. Or even later.

Adam's lips quivered as he spoke. "Mom's death set me back, and I started drinking, but this time I was able to nip it in the bud. I found a psychiatrist who diagnosed me as bipolar and prescribed the appropriate meds. I got myself together, but life...well, my career...didn't pan out. I knew I wasn't suited to engineering, so after sticking it out for two years, I started experimenting with other careers. Data analyst. Website Designer. Car salesman. Bartender. I was all over the map. An advanced case of Career ADD."

"Did you get any career counseling?" I asked, wondering how he could have wandered on so many detours.

"I think I saw every type of counselor." His eyebrows beetled. "Not sure if I ever met a career counselor."

"You're looking at one."

His eyes widened in surprise. "Did you leave teaching?"

I ran through my standard explanation about the lottery win and the ensuing changes in my life. His eyes

56

practically popped out of their sockets as I spoke of the nineteen million dollar win and trips to five continents. His expression grew more pensive at the mention of my growing ReCareering business.

"So, you help people figure out what they want to do." He stroked his chin as he shook his head. "I could have used that advice fifteen years ago. It would have saved me a lot of grief as I worked at those evil day jobs."

There it was again. The famous expression that seemed to have emerged in the last little while. Not sure where the expression originated, but I would say I've heard it dozens of times in the last few months.

"You could have chatted with your guidance counselor or visited the Career office at U of W," I said.

He rolled his eyes. "Mrs. Tompkins wouldn't have had a clue. And I don't think I was ready to listen. My math and science teachers were applauding my choice of an engineering career. Even Mom seemed to approve. Definitely a first."

Two decades ago, Adam had been overjoyed when I selected him as co-editor of the yearbook. For once, he would have an opportunity to shine in a different arena, one Jake would never deign to enter. When the yearbook came out during the last week of June, Adam and Sarah had basked in the praise of their classmates, other teachers on staff, and the principal. I never did find out how his parents responded. A man of few words, Mr. Coburn would have nodded in approval and said, "Well done!" As for Mrs. Coburn, I hoped she would have shown some positive emotion.

I had a brain wave. Why not have Adam come to Sudbury and take advantage of my career services?

When I broached the subject, his eyes lit up. "You mean go through tests and interviews with you?"

"I could administer some of the interest inventories, but I think you might be better served with one of the other counselors on staff for the interviews. They would be more objective." In my mind, I had already paired him off with Mel Nelson. Street-smart and practical, she would serve as the perfect foil for Adam.

He nodded. "I could come up for a day."

"Why not stay longer? My mother's house is vacant right now. She's spending six months in Italy." I paused, wondering if I should address his present state of employment. I hadn't had time to ask Cassandra, and I didn't want to embarrass Adam.

"It's a slow time in the office. Dad will be off on his winter break. I don't think Jake would mind if I took a week off." He shrugged. "To be truthful, I wouldn't mind getting away from the paperwork. And I could use a break from my online courses."

I didn't like the sound of him working in the accounting office. Or of him needing Jake's permission to take a week off. "What courses are you taking?"

"Accounting, Finance. All that business stuff. I promised Dad I'd give it a shot."

"Are you enjoying the courses?" An excellent student, Adam would have no problems absorbing the course content and performing well on all assessments, but I doubted his heart was in this new career direction.

"They're okay," he said in a voice devoid of any enthusiasm. "I'll be ready to write the CA exams next year."

I reached for my purse and rummaged through it

for my business card. "Let me know when you're ready to come," I said as I handed him the card.

As he fingered the card, a thoughtful expression came over his face. "I'll check with Hannah. She might be able to swing a few days as well."

"Hannah…Hannah Biltmore?" I asked. Was he dating Mellow Barbie? I recall him—along with the other boys in the class—admiring her back in Grade Eight, but she never took any of them seriously. Not even Jake. But apparently, everything changed during her senior year at high school. Or maybe she had harbored a secret crush but didn't want to compete with Kaitlin.

"Yeah," he blushed. "We've been going together. It's…uh…getting pretty serious." He sat up straighter. "I can see myself marrying and starting a family with her. And giving her an extra hand with Dougie."

Clanging bells chimed in my ears. He was working with his brother, going out with his brother's ex-girlfriend, and helping with the parenting of his brother's child. Wannabe Ken had returned, ready to settle in a familiar childhood role.

Chapter 9

The doorbell rang. Three successive rings and then the door opened to admit two familiar looking men. Daniel Charette and Bob Wells. I would have recognized them anywhere. Taller and broader than during their Grade 8 year, they sported similar haircuts and clothing styles. Daniel's hair was a dark brown while Bob's could be described as dirty blond. As soon as they spotted me, they rushed over and hugged me.

"*Très belle*, Mademoiselle," Daniel said, twirling me around in a dance move.

"Ditto," Bob added as he winked.

The twosome had been inseparable in Grade Eight. Some days, they even dressed alike. When I implemented a new seating plan, I had contemplated separating them, but I decided not to risk it and was rewarded by grateful glances. To be fair, they gave me no problems. Always respectful, with their homework completed, they were ideal students, scoring consistent Bs in their tests and assignments.

We sat and got caught up. I learned both men were partners in a computer leasing business in Barrie. In their late twenties, they had married two best friends and started families. Daniel had two boys and a girl while Bob had two boys. I oohed and aahed as pictures flashed on their smart phones. Out of the corner of my right eye, I noticed Adam looking bored and restless. It must be difficult for him to sit and listen while two of his classmates shared their family and work successes.

The doorbell rang again. A tall, stunning blonde pushed open the door and entered. Wearing black Lululemon workout gear and flip flops, she appeared effortlessly chic. Her skin glowed from a recent workout; her limbs were long and toned; her thick blond ponytail was threaded through a Blue Jays baseball cap. Hannah or Kaitlin? I couldn't be sure and waited for clues from one of the men.

Before anyone could speak, Adam rose and rushed over. He hugged the woman—who must be Hannah—tightly and kissed her on the mouth. A lingering kiss, much too long and not for public viewing. Or perhaps that was his intention.

"Get a room," Bob muttered as he exchanged glances with Daniel.

I agreed but chose to say nothing. Instead, I stood and waited for Hannah to approach.

She favored me with one of her toothy smiles. "It's so wonderful to see you again, Gilda. I've thought of you often." She reached out and shook my hand. No hugs from Hannah. But that had never been her style.

"Gilda's invited us to Sudbury," Adam said in an excited voice. "We can stay at her Mom's place. We could go in December and take in some snowshoeing and cross country skiing."

"Sounds like a plan. I'll check my schedule at work." Hannah's smile dimmed, only a fraction of a millimeter. The men wouldn't have caught it. I also took note of how she had broken off the embrace first and was now standing apart from Adam.

"Hannah teaches figure skating," Adam explained

as he moved closer and wrapped his arm around her shoulders. "Isn't she in great shape?" He kissed her on the cheek.

"Stop it, Adam Coburn! You're embarrassing me." She pulled away and composed herself. "Dougie said you took pictures at the game."

"Ah, yes," Adams said as he took out his smart phone.

She grabbed it and scrolled through the pictures. Her face softened, and she bit her lip as she gazed at the small phone screen. "His best game ever and I couldn't make it."

"Ten baskets," Adam said.

I waited until Hannah glanced up from the screen. "May I see the pictures?"

Hannah came over and sat beside me. Her voice vibrated with pride as she pointed out her son. I nearly gasped. Dougie was the spitting image of Jake. To be truthful, I couldn't see any bits of Hannah's DNA. In the final picture, father and son stood proudly side-by-side. Dougie was already half-a-head taller than Jake. Definitely a basketball star in the making.

I squeezed Hannah's arm. "You must be so proud."

Her eyes watered as she spoke. "He's the best thing that ever happened to me."

"What is he—" Before I could ask more questions about Dougie, the door opened, and Jake entered, followed by what I could only describe as a handsome Silver Fox. The Fox sported a spiky Anderson Cooper haircut that framed a tanned square-jawed face and dark eyes. At a distance, he could pass for a taller Richard Gere, my long-time celebrity crush.

Jake nodded in everyone's direction. The Fox

followed and glanced around the room. He caught my gaze—and then smiled. "Gilda. Gilda Greco, is that you?"

A familiar voice, one I had heard recently. And then it came to me. The Silver Fox was none other than Constable Leo Mulligan. But unlike the previous evening, the brusque voice was gone, and he was smiling at me. I was not prepared for this particular incarnation of the arrogant playboy I had dated two decades earlier. He had evolved from the Black Irish looks of his early thirties to this mellow, urbane man who was prepared to participate in a psychic-hosted reunion. I wouldn't be too surprised to learn he drank herbal teas and practiced yoga.

He strode toward me, hand outstretched. I shook it and hoped my grip was strong enough to match his. He surveyed the room. "We're missing two people."

Jake spoke up. "Cassandra is upstairs, centering herself. And...and..." He glanced around the room.

"Kaitlin texted she would be running late," Hannah said as she shook her ponytail. "One of the teachers in Orillia invited her to dinner."

"Is that where she lives?" I was surprised to hear Kaitlin Fraser had settled in another small Ontario town. I could still recall her plans to pursue a television career in New York. At the time, Diane Sawyer and Barbara Walters were her role models.

"She lives here in Parry Sound," Hannah explained. "She was invited to present one of her workshops at a Professional Development Day in Orillia."

"She's a teacher?" I asked, hoping I didn't sound too surprised. A worthy profession, and one I had enthusiastically pursued, but I couldn't imagine Kaitlin in that role. At least not the Kaitlin I remembered.

"She teaches Grade Seven." Hannah winked. "But she has ambitions to move up the ladder. She's working on her principal's papers."

Was she married? Did she have children? I would have liked more details but didn't want to appear too nosy in front of the men. The men had moved on to other topics of conversation. Leo was listening intently as Bob and Daniel chatted about gigabytes and smart phones. Techie conversations that could go on for hours.

Hannah rose and approached Jake, who was unloading several wine bottles near the entrance of the dining room. I strained to catch bits of the conversation.

"He was a speed demon," Jake said. "Arms and legs in perfect sync. I chatted with his coach afterward. Terry thinks Dougie could get into a winter basketball camp in Orlando. It's the week right before Christmas. I don't know if—"

"No worries," Hannah said. "It's pretty slow right before Christmas. I'm sure I can get the time off." No hesitation or talk of checking schedules.

Jake raised his eyebrows in surprise. "I can come down, but I won't be able to stay until the end of the camp. It's cutting too close to Christmas, and I don't want to get stuck down there in case there's a Nor'easter along the coast."

Hannah shrugged. "If it's stormy along the coast, I'll stay there for Christmas."

"What about your parents?" Jake asked.

"Maybe I can talk them into coming down," Hannah said. "Make it a family Christmas."

Her eyes never left Jake's as she spoke. All Hannah cared about was her son and his father. Everyone else was color, some Technicolor, some black-and-white, some shades of gray. I suspect Adam fell into the latter category, and I wouldn't be too surprised if he weren't included in the Christmas invitation. Hannah would be content to spend the holiday with her son and elated on the days Jake joined them. Over two decades had passed, and she still hadn't gotten over Jake.

Adam had joined the other men, still deep in tech talk. As I rose to join them, a car horn honked several times.

"Kaitlin's here," Hannah called out.

"So, she announces herself now," Bob said as Daniel poked him in the ribs.

Bob and Daniel versus Kaitlin. A vague memory of raised voices and menacing looks came to mind. But I couldn't recall the details. Hopefully, there would be no drama this evening.

Within seconds, the door opened, and a tall, statuesque blonde entered the room. Kaitlin wore her ash blond hair in a medium length bob. The color was lighter, much lighter than I recalled, but it worked well with her porcelain skin and well-made-up Arctic blue eyes. Of the three Barbies, she was the only one who sported the baby blues. Dressed in a black pantsuit with an ivory-colored blouse, she appeared every inch the administrator she aspired to be. All except for the black patent stilettos, more suited to an evening on the town. I wondered how she could teach all day in heels and then I recalled she had presented a workshop at a Professional Development Day conference in Orillia.

Driving in those high heels would also be a challenge. I suspect she wore comfortable shoes to drive and changed to heels before making her grand entrance. One hour of standing—tops—and then she would need to sit for a while. At least, that was my limited experience with high heels. Having recently given them up, I still glanced longingly at any woman who could walk gracefully in them.

"Mrs...uh...Gilda," she said as she walked toward me. "I was thrilled to hear you would be here today. You were my role model, you know. I admired you so much during those seven months." She waved to include everyone in the room. "You transformed a group of hoodlums into mature, well-behaved students, and you prepared us so well for high school." She hugged me and whispered, "Come over for lunch tomorrow. We need to talk."

Before I could reply, I caught sight of Cassandra walking down the stairs. Dressed in a flowered kimono, with her hair cascading around her shoulders, she faced straight ahead as Jake propelled her toward a room that had remained closed.

Hannah motioned for us to follow. The men rose and followed. Kaitlin and I walked behind them. No one spoke. It felt like we were in some kind of trance or cult. I wondered if this was a normal ritual and if the others had attended séances before.

Chapter 10

We entered what was intended to be a dining room, and probably served that function for most of the time. Tonight, the room was set up for a séance. No electric lights of any kind, only nine unlit cream-colored candles in gold candle holders, arranged around a large mound at the center of an oblong table. Approaching, I picked up the tantalizing aroma of fresh bread. I hadn't seen a bread machine in the kitchen, but then I hadn't taken stock of all the appliances. Had the bread baked while Cassandra was cloistered upstairs? And would we eat it later? While I felt satiated, I could find room in my stomach for a slice or two of freshly baked bread.

Nine chairs were arranged around the table—one at each end, three on one side and four on the other. Cassandra picked one end of the table and motioned Leo toward the other. Jake whispered something to Bob and Daniel who nodded and followed him to the other side of the table. Jake sat to Cassandra's right, followed by Bob, and then Daniel. Adam walked around Leo and sat to his left. All the men on one side. Interesting!

Cassandra motioned toward us. Hannah, Kaitlin and I followed and sat on Cassandra's left. I ended up next to Leo and across from Adam. Adam smiled, and Leo took my hand and squeezed it. While I hadn't known what to expect, I didn't realize I'd feel so unsettled. Perhaps I should have researched séances before coming.

Once we were all seated, Jake rose and lit all the candles. His face remained serious and impassive throughout the process. I noticed the same level of seriousness in everyone else's gaze.

"We shall begin," Cassandra said in a low, confident voice. "First, I must ensure that all present believe it is possible to communicate with Sarah McHenry. If there any non-believers in the room, please leave now." She paused and waited.

I wondered about my skepticism, but I couldn't classify myself as a true non-believer. I wanted, and I'm certain everyone else in the room wanted, to find out what happened to Sarah.

Satisfied, Cassandra continued. "We will now join hands and keep them joined throughout the session."

I felt Kaitlin's tight grip and Leo's more relaxed grip. I wondered about the strength of my grip and if I would be able to keep my hands joined for the entire session. How long did a séance last? What if the spirit didn't come?

"Our beloved Sarah, we bring you gifts from life into death," Cassandra said. "Commune with us, Sarah, and move among us."

Several seconds passed, and Jake repeated, "Our beloved Sarah, we bring you gifts from life into death. Commune with us, Sarah, and move among us."

More silence and then Jake nodded in Hannah's direction. She repeated the summons and waited several more seconds before turning to Kaitlin, who followed suit. As soon as Kaitlin finished speaking, the candle closest to her and Hannah fell. Kaitlin gasped and dropped her hand. I heard another gasp from Hannah.

Both women paled as the flame caught on the fabric of the tablecloth.

Jake reached over and extinguished the candle.

"Welcome, Sarah," Cassandra said. "We are happy you could join us. Kaitlin and Hannah, please join hands and connect with the group."

I felt Kaitlin's moist hand, the grip even tighter.

Cassandra continued, "Sarah, we mourn your absence in our lives. Know that you are loved dearly and missed by all of us—your parents, siblings, and friends. I will ask you simple questions, requiring either a yes or no answer. You can choose to communicate directly using your beautiful voice." Cassandra paused.

Thankfully, not a sound. I wasn't prepared to hear Sarah's voice. The dropped candle had been enough confirmation for Cassandra, and the other two women were shaken up. But I wondered if there was a logical explanation for the candle. Perhaps it wasn't secured properly in the holder. But I didn't want to voice these concerns, lest I be considered a non-believer.

I glanced toward Leo, who was watching Kaitlin and Hannah closely. Did he suspect them of foul play? I couldn't imagine that scenario, but then I wondered at the selection of tonight's participants. We were here for a reason. I assumed mine was to observe and possibly trigger some relevant memory. Cassandra was facilitating, and Leo was also observing. Did that mean the other six had been involved in Sarah's death? Or knew of circumstances leading to her death? I hoped it was the latter situation.

Two more candles toppled over, their tips pointing in Hannah's and Kaitlin's direction. Jake moved quickly to extinguish the flames. Hannah screamed.

Kaitlin yelled out, "Jesus Christ! She's really here...Sarah, speak to us. What happened? Did someone hurt you?" And then "Yow!" She let go of my hand and Hannah's. "Someone kicked me!" Shaken, she looked to Cassandra for guidance.

Bob snickered.

Kaitlin hissed as she turned toward Bob, "So mature of you, Clearasil."

"You deserved it, Meanie," Bob said, winking at Daniel. "This isn't your show, you know. Or maybe it is, and you're not telling us."

Kaitlin leaned over to punch his arm.

Bob pushed back his chair. "You wanna take this outside, Meanie?"

"Stop it!" Leo's voice echoed throughout the room. "This is serious business here. And you're both interfering with a murder investigation."

"He started it," Kaitlin said. She turned to me and added, "This is how he behaved whenever you turned your back or went to help someone else. He wouldn't leave me alone."

"Don't flatter yourself," Bob said. "You started all of this...uh...when..." His face reddened, and he started breathing heavily.

I recalled the incident that had triggered all this animosity. It had not occurred on my watch, but earlier in the year on a supply teacher's last day. According to one of the other teachers, Bob had a crush on Hannah and liked to wander by her desk. On one of Kaitlin's off days—when she assumed her full Meanie self—she lost patience, and on Bob's third stroll around the classroom, she yelled, "What are you—a poster boy for Clearasil? Cut it out and sit down."

The class roared while a mortified Bob made his way to his desk. After that painful incident, he kept his distance, but he didn't hesitate to snarl whenever Kaitlin walked by and she, in turn, would address him as Clearasil.

I was horrified the first time I heard the moniker and chastised Kaitlin. The second time I heard Kaitlin whisper it, I kept her in at recess and made her write a letter of apology to Bob. Part of me wanted Kaitlin to read the letter aloud, sending the message to the rest of the class that nicknames were unacceptable. But I decided to spare Bob the added embarrassment and reminder. Instead, I had Bob and Kaitlin stay in at lunch time. Kaitlin read her letter, and both children shook hands.

Even though I didn't hear "Clearasil" for the rest of the year, I assumed seeds of animosity had been sown. But I had not expected the bitterness to linger this long.

"The circle is broken," Cassandra said, her eyes brimming with tears. "I...I can't continue." She rose and fled the room.

Leo turned on the lights, while Jake blew out the candles.

Leo addressed Kaitlin and Bob. "You both know how important it is for Cassandra to have no distractions and unnecessary noise, let alone immature behavior, during a séance." His jaw clenched as he nodded in Jake's direction. "How secure were those candles?"

"I checked them before everyone entered the room," Jake replied. "They were all tight."

Leo addressed the rest of us. "Did anyone see any hands go down before the candles fell?"

We all shook our heads.

"We can conclude Sarah was here, and she was focusing on Kaitlin and Hannah." Leo scratched his head. "We'll have another séance tomorrow. I'll see if Cassandra can—"

Groans erupted throughout the room.

Daniel spoke up. "Leo, Bob and I are busy with the kids all day. It's Saturday. We've got skating, swimming, and all kinds—"

"Too bad your buddy didn't consider all of that before he decided to kick Kaitlin." Leo crossed his arms. "I guess it'll have to be in the evening again. Anyone not able to make it for seven tomorrow night?"

Resigned faces all around. I surmised that no one had any real excuse and even if they did, didn't want to further anger Leo.

I had promised Carlo I would only spend one night in Parry Sound, but other than that, I didn't have an excuse. But I did wonder why Leo was so insistent on everyone attending. Before leaving tonight, I would touch base with him.

"Gilda, you okay with seven o'clock?" Leo asked, his eyes meeting mine.

"I can stay another day." What else could I say?

Chapter 11

Bob and Daniel left first. I imagine they weren't looking forward to their hour-long drive to Barrie and two more hours on the road tomorrow. Thankfully, it was still autumn, and there was no snow or ice on the roads.

Adam waited until Hannah finished speaking with Kaitlin. He put his arm around Hannah and guided her out the door. I wanted to say goodbye to Cassandra, but I was too late. She had already gone upstairs. Jake and Leo were deep in conversation. I waited for them to finish and started walking toward Leo. I needed to get some answers before tomorrow night's séance.

I felt a pull on my arm. Kaitlin leaned over and whispered, "Hannah will join us tomorrow during her lunch hour. Here's my address." She handed me a business card with handwriting on the back. I tucked the card in my pocket and nodded.

Leo waited until Kaitlin left the room. He laughed. "I had heard about this motley crew, but I didn't realize how bad they must have been. You had your work cut out for you back then." He shook his finger at me. "I'm surprised you didn't jump in and reprimand them."

"You didn't give me a chance," I said. "And I wasn't in charge here."

He gave a quick, impatient shake of his head. "Cassandra needs what we like to call a hot house environment to function as a psychic. Not too practical, especially with this crowd."

"And talking about this crowd," I said, "I need more details...more back story."

"I'm surprised you didn't ask last night," Leo said, raising his eyebrows. "I could have given you the low down on why each person in the room has a reason for being here."

What could I say? I didn't like his tone last night. I hoped one séance would be enough to either solve the mystery of Sarah's death or put an end to my involvement. I shrugged. "I didn't take it too seriously last night."

"And now?" he asked.

"Well, now I guess I'm in the thick of it."

Jake came over. He rubbed his hand over his eyes—a sure sign he was tired. "I'm going to call it a night. If you two want to stay—"

"We'll go," Leo said, glancing at his watch. "I know a famous eating place that's open all hours and will be deserted about now."

"Tim Hortons," I said as he nodded in agreement. "Where's the closest one?"

"Just a couple of blocks away. Follow me in your car." He walked toward the door.

I said goodbye to Jake and followed Leo out the door.

We took our separate cars and reached the Tim Hortons within minutes. Two other patrons were in the restaurant, both in their late teens and very much into each other. I ordered a decaf coffee, and Leo had a Café Mocha. I followed him to a table at the far end, away from the amorous couple and the front counter.

"We can talk here," Jake said as he sipped his coffee.

Up close, I could see the crinkles around his dark eyes and some faded age spots, but he still looked hot. If I weren't involved with Carlo, I would definitely consider going out with him. Thoughts of Carlo brought back the promise he had elicited from me. I couldn't back out of the next séance, and anyway I wouldn't be calling or receiving any calls from Carlo tonight. This time tomorrow night, I could be on my way back to Sudbury. Séance Number Two would either bring forth more information or end my involvement. I couldn't imagine Leo ordering a third séance.

"Ask away," Leo said, leaning back in his chair.

So many questions whirled in my mind. And I would have time to ask them. I took a deep breath. "I want to know why those particular six people were invited."

"First of all, Cassandra's a bit superstitious and likes to conduct séances with groups that are multiples of three. After the three of us had been confirmed, she asked Jake, who participates whenever she needs an extra person."

"Was that his only role?" I asked, stirring my coffee. "To be a placeholder?"

Leo's eyes widened. "What are you suggesting?"

"Well, it's no secret that Jake liked to flirt with all the girls, especially the Barbies. Sarah McHenry was a Barbie."

"Moody Barbie," Leo said. "The name still suits…uh…suited her. She had some wild mood swings. She was diagnosed with bipolar depression when she was still in high school. I think she was okay as long as she took her meds."

"She wasn't taking her meds?" I asked, hoping and praying Adam was more compliant.

"Her mother seemed to think she was. Her father...well...her father never did put too much stock in taking pills. Living with him again, she might have stopped."

Another one who had moved back home. While I would have liked to hear more details about Sarah's home life, I suspect I'd get more precise information from Kaitlin and Hannah tomorrow at lunch.

"Back to Jake," I said. "Do you think he might have...well...uh flirted with Sarah? Maybe led her to believe there could be something more between them."

"Hmm. Not sure. But I do know she pursued him."

"What?" I wasn't prepared for that response. Thinking back, I recalled Kaitlin being more aggressive while both Hannah and Sarah hung back.

"Oh, yes," Leo said, shaking his head. "And she didn't stop there. She propositioned all of them—Jake, Adam, Bob, Daniel—and then moved beyond her circle of friends and acquaintances."

I tried not to show my shock and sadness. Sarah had probably stopped taking her meds and moved into a manic stage. She wasn't responsible for her behavior. Hopefully, the men had recognized her vulnerable state and disengaged themselves. I'd like to think that my former students had evolved into kind and considerate men, who would not take advantage of a mentally ill woman.

Having fought his own demons, Adam would have empathy. And I couldn't imagine him two-timing Hannah. He was besotted with her and already planning their future together. But I got a very different vibe from Hannah this evening. In her heart of hearts, she was still mooning over Jake. At some level, she was probably hoping he'd leave Cassandra.

Cassandra was very much in love with Jake, and Jake—well, I didn't think he felt quite the same way. At least, that's the impression I got this evening. While he gave Cassandra a quick peck on the cheek, he spent more time chatting with Hannah and me. Jake was the beloved in that relationship. But, and a very big but, I could imagine him straying. Having a fling to test his attractiveness was a real possibility. One I hope he didn't indulge in too often. And if he did, he did so discreetly. But was that even possible when married to a psychic?

Bob and Daniel. While teaching them, I got a gay vibe. I don't know if I was extra-sensitive after Luigi's betrayal, but I felt the two of them were enmeshed. And then I recalled Bob's crush on Hannah. As for Daniel, he was the yin member of the partnership. He said very little and raised his voice tonight only when Leo scheduled the second séance. I suspect the others had similar sentiments. To be truthful, I wasn't looking forward to more dropped candles. If that's all that happened during a séance, was it even worth having another one?

"You don't want it to be any of them," Leo said in a low voice. "And neither do I. But someone pushed Sarah McHenry down that hill, and it's my job to apprehend that person."

"You said Sarah moved beyond tonight's circle. Who else did she approach?"

A wary, concerned expression crossed his face

before he quickly smoothed it away. "Who didn't she approach might be an easier question to answer. Let's just say she phoned, emailed, or cozied up to any man from her past or...or who she happened to meet during her nightly visits to local watering holes."

"She was off her meds and drinking?"

Leo shrugged. "Not sure if she was or wasn't taking her meds. Her parents are pretty mum about her mental health. But I have it on good authority that she spent her nights off at local bars."

"Where did she work?"

"She was a waitress at one of the sports bars in Barrie," Leo said. "While she was on the job, she was sober. The customers all liked her, and she got good tips."

I knew of many artists, writers and other creatives who preferred to wait tables or bartend in the evenings, leaving their days free for creative pursuits. I hoped Sarah had not abandoned her art. It would be a shame to let all that talent go to waste.

Leo yawned and stretched his arms. "I'm pretty beat. Anything else you want to know?"

"How do Kaitlin and Hannah figure in all of this? Are you including them because of their friendship with Sarah?"

"Sarah had a falling out with Kaitlin about two months ago. I don't know what Sarah was thinking when she propositioned Wayne—Kaitlin's husband—while he was grilling burgers on the deck. One of the other guests overheard and told Kaitlin. Sparks flew with over twenty people in attendance. Hannah tried to stay neutral, but she eventually sided with Kaitlin."

"So, Sarah's been alone for a while."

Leo's eyes flashed with what looked like annoyance. "I wouldn't jump to that conclusion. There were several other calls on her phone. Some of the visitors to our fair town did return her affections. We're tracing those calls right now."

"So, it could be an outsider." Why on earth was Leo bothering with a séance?

"It could, but I think it's a local." He paused. "And Cassandra agrees."

"She suspects someone."

Leo nodded but said nothing.

"But she's not sharing."

More nodding. Leo rose and donned his jacket.

"One other thing," I said as I stood. "Everyone seemed to know what to do at the séance. It's like you were all programmed beforehand."

Leo laughed. "Not quite. We've all attended at least one séance since Cassandra's....uh...I guess you can call it a transformation. When my dad passed away, Mom and I asked for one. Some of the others lost grandparents, uncles, and aunts. It's what we do here in Parry Sound."

Leo accompanied me to my car. "One more thing. I need to apologize for my behavior at our...well, I guess that was a date. I was a total jerk, and I'm sorry if I upset you."

"I wasn't very co-operative either." Thinking back, I could have listened and made the occasional kind comment. I didn't have to turn him off and act like the evening was torture.

"And here we are again," Leo said, coming closer. "Two decades later and I'm single again. Wife Number Three left about a year ago."

"Three wives?" I shook my head in amazement. I had heard of police officers being difficult husbands, but somehow the marriages survived those rocky patches.

"What about you?" Leo asked, ignoring my comment.

"I'm involved with someone." I decided not to share too much about Carlo. Their paths might have crossed. And to be truthful, I wasn't too sure about our future together. All that West Coast talk was started to grate on my nerves.

"Figured," he said. He gave me a bear hug and walked toward his car.

Would he have asked me out if I was available? For one brief moment, I considered the possibility of having a do-over date with Leo Mulligan aka Leo the Hunk aka evolved Silver Fox.

Chapter 12

Nine-forty. I was exhausted but also wired. If I got into bed now, I would toss and turn for hours. It was still early, but I didn't want to go out alone in a town where I was liable to run into a former student, parent, or resident who would recognize me. I needed space from tonight's participants. I thought of my friends and colleagues from the past. Calling one of them now would necessitate too many explanations. And while Parry Sound was small and news traveled quickly, I hoped not too many people had heard of my connection to Sarah McHenry's death.

Carlo was on Vancouver Island, living it up with his children and grandchildren. It was six-forty there, smack in the middle of family dinner, a joyous event that would delight Carlo. Not a good time to tear him away and deliver more unsettling news. He had mentioned calling me Saturday night. Why borrow trouble and upset him by telling him I would have to stay for a second séance?

Another name and number came to mind. One I didn't use too often, but I knew he would be willing to listen. Would he be home at nine-forty on a Friday night in Sudbury? I took out my cell and scrolled through until I located the number.

He answered on the third ring. "Gilda Greco calling me on a Friday night. I can only come up with two possible scenarios, one very unlikely and another one much more predictable."

"Humor me. What do you consider an unlikely scenario?"

"You have seen the light and decided to break up with your boyfriend." He lowered his voice. "And you'd like to test the waters with me."

I burst into loud laughter, and he joined in. The thought of starting a relationship with Jim Nelson was beyond unlikely. It bordered on ludicrous. Nothing against Jim, but we were polar opposites who had nothing in common but somehow managed to work well together in spite of those differences. I harbored no romantic interest, and I knew he was just as detached from me.

I had met Jim two years ago when I was considered the prime suspect in a series of murders. Even Carlo had his doubts as one dead blonde after another mysteriously appeared in a Dumpster near one of my favorite haunts. Each time, I lacked an alibi. At first hostile and uncooperative, Jim came around, and I hired him as a private investigator.

We developed an easy rapport that morphed into light banter. It helped that I had hired his daughter Mel as receptionist at ReCareering, where she was flourishing

Six months ago, I called Jim to help with a second set of murders. Without his diligent and persistent probing, I don't think the case would have been solved as quickly. There was only one major obstacle. He and Carlo didn't see eye-to-eye on many issues. At first, I had assumed my initial interference in the four murders had caused the rift. But I learned later that the two men had been on the outs since high school. Unbelievable how those high school scuffles can cut across the decades. Those of us who left Sudbury managed to put the past behind us, but those who remained hadn't been able to escape their histories. The same could be said about my former students in Parry Sound.

Jim groaned. "It must be the usual. You're chasing another ambulance. Where'd you find the body this time?"

He had my number, in more ways than one. "I didn't chase this body." I gave him a summary of the last twenty-four hours.

Jim whistled. "You sure don't like it easy. With all your millions, you'd think this crap could somehow miss landing on you. But you do seem to attract it." He chuckled. "Might be something to address with a therapist or maybe the psychic you've just met."

"I didn't just meet her. I got to know her and her parents very well during those seven months I taught in Parry Sound. They're good people." While I was also skeptical, I did feel the urge to defend her. She had been so sincere and so open. I couldn't fathom the notion of Cassandra faking or putting on the airs of a psychic. It wasn't in her nature to be deceitful.

"I'm sure they are," Jim said. "But let's face some facts here. Most psychics need to make a living. I don't doubt this lady has some intuitive ability—as many women do—but I don't think it's enough to catch a murderer. The constable is grasping at straws. What did you say his name was?"

"Leo. Leo Mulligan."

"Tall, dark-haired guy. Good-looking and a bit of a rascal."

"He's evolved." I immediately regretted my response. Knowing Jim, he would pounce and tease me.

"And you're interested," Jim said, chuckling. "What does your boyfriend think about this cozy reunion you're having?"

"He's not too happy about my involvement." I tried not to think of how Carlo would react to my staying in Parry Sound for a second séance. "He's helping his daughter relocate to Vancouver. I don't know when he'll be back." Ten days, maximum, he had said. And already two weeks had passed. He was close to retirement and would have no problems extending his break.

"When the cat's away—"

"Stop it, Jim! There's nothing going on between Leo and me." I regretted calling Jim and had half a mind to hang up. I composed myself and tried to modulate my voice. "I'm calling to ask for your help. I don't think tomorrow's séance will reveal anything too earth-shattering, and I'm hoping Leo won't suggest a third séance. But I do think there's some foul play here. I'd hate to see this become one of those cold cases tucked away in the back of a filing cabinet. At the very least, I can help by hiring you to investigate the people in Sarah's life." Knowing Jim, he would investigate each name I mentioned.

"Do you have a specific timeline in mind?"

In my heart of hearts, I wanted to see everything tidied up this weekend. But was that even possible? "Let's take it one day at a time."

"Hmm," Jim sighed. "I'm going to set a timeline of a week. Start by giving me the full names of everyone you met tonight."

I rattled off the names and waited while he wrote them down.

"Coburn…any relation to Peggy?"

"You mean Margaret Coburn?" The thought of Jim and Margaret being so familiar with each other was mind-boggling. If I were still teaching, I would be tempted to share this tidbit with my colleagues who were in awe of Margaret.

"That's the one," he said. "She hired me for a few jobs."

"Margaret Coburn hired you to investigate?" Prim and proper, the woman maintained her distance with everyone outside her immediate family. And even there, she focused primarily on Jake. Adam was an after-thought. As for Douglas Coburn, he simply accompanied her.

"Sure did," Jim said. "And she met with me here in Sudbury."

Another incongruent event. Each time I visited Jim's office I was greeted by general disorder and lack of cleanliness. Files were piled up on the reception desk, chairs, and on the floor nearby. The wastepaper basket overflowed with coffee cups, plastic wrap, and food. Where on earth had fastidious Margaret Coburn sat? Elegantly dressed in soft pastels and pearls, she would have wrinkled her nose in disgust and perhaps chosen to stand throughout their appointment.

"Believe it or not, she didn't notice her surroundings." He chuckled. "I had a steady receptionist back then who kept everything ship-shape."

Why would Margaret Coburn hire Jim Nelson? While I had every confidence in Jim, I couldn't imagine Margaret going out of her way to hire him. If she needed an investigator, I would have thought she'd call someone in Toronto. Her parents and siblings lived in southern Ontario. I wasn't sure where, but they would have access to more private investigators in metropolitan areas.

"You're itching to ask." Jim paused. "If I feel it's relevant to the unfortunate death of the young woman, I'll let Mulligan know. But to be truthful, I don't recall all the details." He lowered his voice. "Gilda, you should be able to figure out why a middle-aged woman would need my services."

Infidelity. I recalled Adam's comment about his parents divorcing. Had Margaret discovered an affair? Or maybe several affairs? Jim had mentioned a few jobs. "A few" meant three or more. At least, that's my interpretation. I would let Jim work at his own pace and discretion. In the past, he had managed to unearth some interesting tidbits. But I had to give him space and not pester him with calls.

"I'll start tomorrow morning," Jim said. "If I find something or need more clarification, I'll call your cell."

"I'll give you a call after I meet with Hannah and Kaitlin." I would get more information about Sarah. Hopefully, some names of past paramours and more recent ones. But I would have to tread carefully. I didn't want either woman to know what Leo had shared. Even if it was public knowledge, I wanted the women to think I was hearing about their spats and skirmishes for the first time. Spats and skirmishes that had succeeded in distancing Sarah from her two best friends and left her vulnerable to foul play.

"Take care, Gilda." Jim hung up.

Seven deaths in two years' time. Was I attracting all this darkness? Or was it happenstance? Might be something to ask Cassandra. But not tomorrow. She would be busy with the holistic fair and would then have to prepare herself for Séance Number Two.

Chapter 13

Saturday, October 26, 2013

I was up an hour before my wake-up call and did yoga stretches. I showered and dressed casually in jeans and a sweatshirt topped by a lightweight jacket. I decided to take advantage of the complimentary breakfast offered by the hotel. Knowing I would have lunch at Kaitlin's, I was fine with toast, cereal, and coffee. I'd have a hot breakfast tomorrow morning.

As I munched on my toast, I noticed the room filling up with groups of women, many of them in their forties and beyond. Could they all be here for a conference? Or perhaps a craft show? Or the Holistic Fair? I waited until two ladies sat at a nearby table, and eavesdropped on their conversation.

"I couldn't sleep a wink. I don't know who was in the room next door, but they seemed to be in and out a lot. And their door didn't close too quietly." The first woman sighed. "I've already complained twice to the twit at the front desk. She rolled her eyes and said she would let the manager know, which is code for 'Forget it, lady.' I'm giving them a negative review on their website, and I'm writing a formal letter of complaint."

"I didn't hear a thing. I took a sleeping pill and was out like a light." The second woman yawned loudly. "I'm still feeling a bit groggy. I could have used an extra hour of sleep."

"No, you couldn't. If this fair is anything like Cassandra's last event, it'll be standing room only for her talk. I don't want to stand way at the back for an hour and have to put up with people jostling me again."

"Relax! It's only eight o'clock. We've got ninety minutes to kill before she starts speaking."

"I'm heading for one of the front rows as soon as we get there. You can do whatever you want."

Standing room only. Saving seats. It sounded like the ladies were getting ready to hear a rock star perform. And, in many ways, Cassandra was a rock star. She had the looks, charisma, compelling back story, and powers. To be truthful, I hadn't seen too much evidence of the latter, but I was open to hearing her speak today. I also had mixed feelings when it came to tonight's séance. Part of me wanted more details about Sarah's death to emerge while another part wanted my involvement to end.

From what Leo had said, Sarah had propositioned many men, some total strangers who were long gone. Any one of them could have pushed Sarah a bit too hard and caused her to fall down the hill. But Cassandra and Leo seemed to think the culprit—I couldn't think of any of them as a cold-blooded murderer—was one of the participants in last night's séance.

Leo seemed to focus on the men, but he hadn't ruled out Kaitlin or Hannah. Could one or both of them have confronted Sarah and taken their skirmish to the next level? Two decades ago, Kaitlin's mean streak had intimidated some of her classmates. Bob, for one, kept his distance and some of the other girls—Big Mouse and Little Mouse—had little to do with her. Aware of these tensions, I ensured Bob, Big Mouse, and Little Mouse were seated at opposite ends of the room. And I didn't hesitate to reprimand Kaitlin whenever she made an inappropriate comment. As for Hannah, I hadn't seen any evidence of meanness. I would have to watch and listen closely at today's luncheon.

The women at the next table rushed out the door. I paid my bill and went to my car.

Within minutes I arrived at the hall and wasn't too surprised to find the parking lot half full. I parked and made my way inside. A small line had formed. So far, all women. Men did attend these events, but they were often outnumbered ten to one. At least that had been my experience in Sudbury and south-western Ontario. I wondered if the ratio would change significantly in the town associated with hockey and Bobby Orr. I can still recall the horrified expressions on my friends' faces when I informed them I would be teaching in Parry Sound.

I laughed at their ridiculous comments: "You'll end up with a hockey player, have kids who play hockey, and spend the rest of your life as a hockey mom and hockey grandma."

"You'll spend your nights and weekends alone."

"Do they have a movie theater, library, or bookstore?"

"We'll have to send you books and magazines and keep you up-to-date with what's happening out in the real world."

I moved up the line and paid seven dollars for the day. Entering the large hall, I was greeted by two young women waving programs and pamphlets. I had almost an hour before Cassandra's lecture, more than enough time to visit some of the booths. As I strolled around the room, I recognized many of the practitioners: personal health coaches, nutritional counselors, acupuncturists, Reiki masters, reflexologists, and shamanic healers.

And, of course, the psychics.

Having attended several Holistic Fairs, I was familiar with many of the modalities. My interest today was with the psychics. In the past, I had smiled and moved along, not wanting to engage or purchase a reading. While I like to think of myself as more evolved than people like Carlo and Jim, who equate psychic ability with hocus-pocus, I was still wary and a bit afraid of what these women would discover if they started reading my cards. Was I afraid to find out why I attracted so many dead bodies?

I stopped at three booths with psychics and spoke to the women. The first woman launched into a spiel about her epiphany at age four. A New Yorker, she spoke quickly, barely pausing to take a breath. "You'll get your money's worth with me. I can out-talk anyone here." She waved her hand around the room.

Out-talk and turn off in the process, I thought. Listening to her for a thirty-minute session would be very stressful, and I doubted I would get any new insights. I took her card and moved on.

The next psychic spouted off a list of credentials and fellowships, focusing on spirit and ministry: Spiritualist Minister, Fellowships of the Spirit School of Healing and Prophecy, Minister in Residence. Her pamphlet mentioned a bachelor's degree in education and experience in dance and yoga instruction. Another advanced case of Career ADD!

At the third booth, Reverend Clarissa stretched out her arms and embraced me. Wearing a long flowing black vest with hints of red flowers over black pants and a black top, she towered over me. Her large poster board showcased her international bestsellers—*The Soul's Plan* and *The Soul's Journey*—leaving only enough room for two piles of pamphlets.

Her eyes locked with mine. "I've been reading Tarot cards and connecting with the Divine for four decades. I can sense your skepticism, but there's a still inner voice yearning for more. You appear to have it all, but you don't really, do you, my dear?"

We're all yearning for more, I wanted to say. But I didn't wish to get into a long discussion and have to explain why I wasn't interested in having a reading. To be truthful, if I wanted a reading I would ask Cassandra. I nodded and took a pamphlet.

Enough browsing. I made my way to the large hall and found an empty seat in the middle section. I wasn't in the front row, but I had an unobstructed view of the stage and would be able to see and hear Cassandra. While waiting, I studied the day's programs. Many of the sessions dealt with energy healing and chakra clearing. Not what I wanted to hear today. My gaze gravitated to "Learn Your Life Purpose" and "Meditation for Physical, Emotional, and Spiritual Wellness." Both workshops would follow Cassandra's talk and take me to the noon hour.

Having checked off my preferences, I tucked the card in my tote and took off my jacket. It was getting warm in the hall.

A familiar male voice broke into my thoughts. "I figured you'd be here."

I glanced up into Leo's dancing eyes. Dressed in jeans and a dark blue sweat shirt, he appeared even hotter today. Silver foxes look oh so good in blues and jewel colors. In fact, I didn't think there were too many colors or styles that wouldn't suit Leo Mulligan. "I didn't think this would be your usual Saturday morning activity."

Leo shook his head. "There's a lot you don't know about me, pretty lady."

And now he was flirting. I didn't mind, not one bit.

Before I could respond, a loud voice interrupted. "Good morning, everyone. Please take your places. We're about to begin."

I was surrounded by a sea of humanity with only a scattering of empty seats. About twenty people, some of them men, stood at the back.

The announcer smiled brightly. "Thank you all for coming. I've heard some of you have come from as far away as upstate New York. We are happy to have you here and hope you will take in all the Fair has to offer. Afterward, take a stroll through the downtown and have lunch at one of the main eateries that we are famous for. Parry Sound is small but has a lot to offer. We are very proud to offer this opportunity to hear Cassandra Coburn share her life journey and the insights she has learned along the way. A special daughter of Parry Sound, she was born and raised here, and then decided to marry her childhood sweetheart and settle amongst us." A few whistles and scattered applause followed.

"Please join me in welcoming Cassandra Coburn."

We all stood and clapped as Cassandra walked across the stage. I had half expected her to wear the flowered kimono, but she was dressed conservatively in black pants with a turquoise blazer and white blouse. She appeared poised and confident. A far cry from the shy, self-conscious teen, and well recovered from last night's debacle.

She opened her arms wide and started speaking. "Welcome old friends and new friends. I can feel your positive energy radiating to the four corners of the room." She paused. "And some negative bits of skepticism, as well." A few titters of laughter. "And that's okay, too. I like challenges."

"Today, I want to talk about using your intuition to solve problems and create miracles. That's right, you're not hearing things. You can all tap into those inner reservoirs and fix whatever needs fixing in your life. In fact, you can get so good at it, you won't need the help of anyone in this room." More laughter.

Cassandra waited for the laughter to subside. She spoke to the practitioners. "Don't worry. You'll be kept busy for today. I don't expect miracles to occur too quickly." Cassandra then waved her hand to include everyone in the audience. "And neither should any of you. Transforming and evolving is a process that can take weeks, months, years, and even decades. So don't despair if you're not seeing too many changes right away. Continue to put one foot in front of the other, and do something different each day."

Everyone's attention focused on Cassandra. They were all hungry for change and willing to listen to any messiah, divine or otherwise. I suspect they considered Cassandra close to divine.

For the next forty minutes, Cassandra shared five strategies that would help anyone tap into their intuition. I had hoped to jot down points but found myself rapt with attention as beautifully articulated fragments reverberated through the room.

"Feel it in your belly, and don't ignore those goose bumps…Release those negative emotions that can cloud intuition…Surround yourself with people who enrich and empower you…Walk away from anyone who drains you…Pay attention to your dreams."

I had heard much of this before, but never so eloquently delivered. I would ask Cassandra to send me a copy of her talk.

Cassandra ended on a dramatic note, quoting from Steve Jobs' famous 2005 commencement address at Stanford.

As soon as the question-and-answer period started, hands went up all around. Two young women with microphones sprinted around the hall, selecting people at random. Most of the questions centered on the mental gremlins that could easily distract and disrupt the best of intentions. Cassandra addressed all the questions, often meeting with applause.

"Last question," one of the female runners shouted as she approached a young woman who appeared to be arguing with her partner.

The young woman grabbed the microphone and shouted, "I want to know why you're stalling the investigation into Sarah McHenry's murder. If you're such an expert and evolved intuitive, you should be able to pinpoint the murderer. Unless…well…are you covering up for someone?"

There was a collective gasp in the audience. One woman shouted, "Sit down, bitch. You're out of line."

Leo swore under his breath. I reached over and squeezed his hand. I was feeling equally indignant and wondering how that young woman had learned about Cassandra's involvement with the investigation. Someone had spilled the beans.

Cassandra didn't miss a beat. She waited for the audience members to settle down. "If you have any concerns or information, please share them with the police."

The young woman persisted. "You've helped solve murders across this country. Are you going to try harder at tonight's séance?"

Leo sprang up and sprinted toward the other runner who was in our section. He took the microphone. "I think Cassandra Coburn answered your first question, young lady. Which, if I recall correctly, was the last question." He waved his hand to include all the audience members. "I would invite anyone who has information about Sarah McHenry's death to contact me. I'm Constable Leo Mulligan, and I can be reached at the local OPP office."

Smooth. Leo had put the interloper in her place and managed to convey he was open to questions and concerns.

Several murmurs could be heard as the event organizer approached the podium. She shook Cassandra's hand and thanked her for taking time out of her busy schedule to share her wisdom with the people of Parry Sound.

After a subdued round of applause, Cassandra left the stage. Audience members rose and made their way toward the booths and eating area. Leo scowled as he scanned the crowd. "She's gone."

"Who was that?" All I could recall was long, black hair on a tall, thin frame.

"I think she's one of the waitresses who worked with Sarah. She's from Orillia…or maybe Midland. I remember talking with her during the investigation."

"How did she find out about last night?"

Leo's eyes sparked with anger. "Someone's squealing. Maybe someone who's not too happy about being coerced into attending a second séance."

Bob and Daniel came to mind first. While they lived in Barrie, I couldn't imagine them stopping at Sarah's restaurant and taking more time out of their long days. After working all day and then attending the séance, they would be anxious to get home and spend time with their families.

I shared my concerns with Leo, who smiled. "Email and texting. Whoever shared did it digitally, and the news spread like wildfire. The waitress probably heard it third or fourth-hand." He glanced at his watch. "I have about two hours before I take my sons to hockey practice. I guess I'll be visiting that restaurant and seeing what I can dig up." He leaned over and hugged me. "Take care, Gilda. See you tonight."

He sauntered toward the door, oblivious to the admiring glances he received. His deep baritone had captured everyone's attention. And his looks had generated discussion, among the locals and visitors. I was certain everyone now knew he was thrice divorced and available.

I felt a poke in my back and jumped. Turning, I caught the dark glances of two women I never expected to see at a Holistic Fair in Parry Sound or anywhere else for that matter: Maria Rossi and Rosa Geraldi, my godmother and her sister.

Chapter 14

"What are you doing here?" If this were any other day, I'd be thrilled to see them. Having known them all my life and spent many hours in their company, I appreciated the interest they took in me. But I had learned from an early age not to over-share. Both sisters possessed the gossip gene and delighted in being the first to share news—good and bad—with the rest of the Italian community in Sudbury, and sometimes their epistles crossed the ocean to Italy. They didn't hesitate to add their own spin on the situation.

"We came as soon as we heard," Maria said.

"Heard what?" I said, trying to keep my emotions from splattering across my face.

Rosa shook a finger at me. "You're involved in another murder. Seven murders since you came back to Sudbury. You're starting to get a reputation as an ambulance chaser."

"How did you hear?" I doubted they were in the same loop as the waitress. Or maybe they were. Maria's granddaughter Belinda, who worked at ReCareering, was active on social media and could have alerted them. But what could be Belinda's connection to Parry Sound?

"Vera Lodestro phoned last night. She told us all about the student who died and how her niece Cassandra is involved...and you...in this mess." Maria shook her head. "Why they had to call you with Carlo out of town is beyond me."

The wheels started turning. Cassandra must have phoned her aunt or maybe the aunt phoned her. And Vera had decided to alert Maria and Rosa. "I didn't know you still stayed in touch."

"Whenever we drive to Toronto, we stop for lunch." Rosa added, raising one finger. "One way only. We don't want to impose."

Maria chuckled as she glanced around the hall. "They're fakes, all of them, even Cassandra."

"Maria!" This was not an appropriate conversation to be having at a holistic fair where dozens of psychics had congregated.

"She's right," Rosa said, waving her hand around the hall. "We stopped to see three of them. All they talk about are their epiphanies and how they can help us. They want to charge eighty dollars for thirty minutes. Who would pay that kind of money?"

Maria nodded. "Those old witches in Italy, especially the ones in Sicily, have all the powers. None of these psychics come close. Not even Cassandra. She's too young and too pretty. You need to be old and ugly to have real powers."

Rosa poked Maria. "We can't say anything to Vera. She'll be offended."

I nodded. "Cassandra is well known across the country. She's helped a lot of people."

"But she couldn't help her friend," Maria said. "She was a…what do you call it…"

"Basket case," Rosa suggested. "Vera said she was crying on the phone and had to take a sedative before falling asleep."

"She recovered today," I said. Was Cassandra in the habit of sharing with her aunt, who also possessed the gossip gene? I recalled the subtle grilling I received whenever I was invited for supper at Vera's. Mostly about Cassandra and how well she was doing at school, but sometimes she would sneak in questions about my non-existent social life. As much as possible, I tried to give evasive answers. I suspected she had the "perfect" man in mind for me, and I wasn't ready to go down that particular road.

"Hmm." Maria put her hands on her hips. "I had to work hard to persuade Vera not to share with any of the relatives in Italy. Your mother just left Sudbury last week. I don't think you want her hopping on the plane and coming back."

I groaned at the thought of news traveling across the ocean. It wouldn't be the first time my mother learned about my involvement in murder investigations while away from Sudbury. This past March, she had cut her stay in Italy short and rushed back when she heard about the Greek Restaurant murders. Was I now starting to give each case a different name? Would this murder end up being the Parry Sound murder? Or maybe the psychic murder?

Maria hugged me. "Don't worry. We've brought wine, salami, Baci Perugina, sauce, and some desserts from Regency Bakery. Vera's happy."

Food gifts. That works with Italians, and I imagine with almost everyone else. Feed people and keep them quiet.

"She's invited the three of us for dinner tonight," Rosa said. "We'll eat early, about five, so you'll have lots of time before the witchcraft."

I winced at the thought of being offered as part bribe and also at the mention of witchcraft. "It's called a séance. Psychics aren't witches."

"What's the difference?" Maria asked but didn't give me a chance to answer. "They meet in dark rooms, use candles, contact spirits, and cast spells."

"They don't cast spells," I said, trying to forget about the trance-like behavior exhibited by the others last night.

"Okay, then," Maria said, rolling her eyes. "They use their powers to get what they want."

"For the common good," I added. I glanced at my watch. In less than five minutes, the first lecture would start.

"We also have plans," Rosa said. "We're having a quick lunch with Vera and then helping prepare for tonight's dinner."

"We'll pray a rosary for this case to be solved." Maria pointed toward the booths. "First, we're going to get our readings."

"But you said you don't believe..." I smiled, recalling one of my mother's favorite sayings: *Chi disprezza, compra.* Whoever criticizes, ends up buying.

"We don't," Maria said. "But we want to see what the old witch...uh...psychic says. The young ones are standing around twiddling their thumbs, but she's getting customers. And she's probably the best of the group. She's old, and she's lost her looks."

"One hundred dollars for two readings," Rosa said. "That's what we'll offer her."

"You can't negotiate here," I said, wanting for several seconds to be a fly on the wall when they approached the septuagenarian, whom I had also noticed earlier. Well-established in the psychic world for almost five decades, she still commanded considerable attention and had a following in Canada and the United States.

"We'll get a deal," Rosa said confidently. "We'll see you later."

Maria lowered her voice. "Be careful around the wolf. People talk. You don't want Carlo hearing that you're keeping company with another man."

"He is handsome but dangerous," Rosa said. "You can see it in those black eyes."

"A devil!" Maria poked me again. "Stay away from him."

Unbelievable! Maria and Rosa didn't miss a thing. But I imagine every other woman in the hall took note of Leo and gave me the once-over.

I spent the next hour listening to two different practitioners talk about finding your life purpose and meditation. While taking notes, I realized most of the information was not new to me. But the physical act of taking notes distracted me from troublesome thoughts about tonight's séance, Leo Mulligan, and the extra wrinkles added by Maria's and Rosa's presence in Parry Sound.

Chapter 15

I didn't need my GPS to find Kaitlin's house. After driving around Parry Sound for almost a day, I started remembering the streets. As I pulled into the driveway, I was both surprised and impressed by the older, restored home. In Grade Eight, she had spoken at length about living in a penthouse condo overlooking Central Park and either walking or taking limos. She had read somewhere that Barbara Walters walked to work each morning and took limos whenever she had to attend a special event.

In spite of its age, the house was beautifully restored. I loved the wraparound verandah—one of my dreams for the perfect home. Interestingly enough, I lived in a condo with a view of Lake Nepahwin, but I still dreamt of living in a house very much like Kaitlin's.

I didn't get a chance to knock. Kaitlin opened the door and ushered me into a lived-in living room. With most of my friends in their fifties and older, I didn't have too many opportunities to visit a home where young children lived. No ice-cream palettes here. Instead, the slate blue walls, patterned sofas and chairs, and velvet stacked floor cushions gave off a classy but comfortable vibe. Casual elegance came to mind.

I didn't notice Hannah until she spoke. "Pretty impressive, isn't it? The house was featured in

Canadian House & Home last year."

Kaitlin made a face. "No biggie." But I could tell she was proud of her home. Had she decorated it herself or hired someone? Having been around relatives and friends in the interior design business, I always marveled at their amazing instincts. They seemed to know what pillows or patterns could be combined to produce a stunning effect. Glancing at the varying shades of blue and competing patterns in this room, I knew I wouldn't have been able to combine those disparate elements.

"Hannah has only an hour, so we'll have to eat right away." Kaitlin sighed. "I hope you're okay eating in the kitchen. The girls left all their craft projects on the dining room table, and I haven't had time to tidy up."

"Are your daughters here?" I was curious about her daughters and choice of husband. The Kaitlin I had known hadn't planned on getting married until well into her thirties. And children weren't even on the radar in Grade Eight.

"They have Daddy-time on Saturdays. Wayne took them to their swimming and gymnastics lessons this morning." Kaitlin frowned. "About now, they're having lunch somewhere I would never take them."

Hannah shook her head. "You need to curtail those visits to fast food places. Once a week is much too often. When they're older, they'll think it's acceptable to treat themselves to those extra calories. And then they'll spiral out of control."

Pushy and rude. I didn't think it appropriate for Hannah to be commenting on how Kaitlin should be raising her children.

Kaitlin winced as she glanced down at her waist. She was wearing baggy sweats and a long top. With her hair tied back and no traces of makeup, she appeared several years older than Hannah, who was wearing another sleek Lululemon outfit. Hannah had applied her makeup with a light hand, and her high pony tail accentuated her sculptured features.

Had Hannah taken the lead in their relationship? I had always considered Kaitlin the instigator and Hannah and Sarah her followers. Kaitlin and Hannah must have switched roles somewhere along the way. And what about Sarah? I could never imagine Sarah assuming any form of leadership role even if she wasn't always willing to go along with whatever Kaitlin suggested. Toward the spring of that year, I noticed Sarah spending more and more time apart from the other two. Granted, she was busy with yearbook deadlines and spent most of her time with Adam. As co-editors, they often met during recesses to discuss the yearbook. And I suspect they met during the evenings. Margaret Coburn wouldn't have minded at all. Wrapped up in Jake's life, she barely acknowledged Adam's presence. Did Margaret even notice that Sarah and Adam attended the Grad dance together?

I was surprised by the large eat-in kitchen with an island and state-of-the-art appliances. An attractive combination of old and new, everything sparkled. While Kaitlin may not have had time to tidy the dining room, she had not neglected her kitchen. She pointed toward a round table that could comfortably seat six, possibly more if a leaf was added.

Kaitlin poured soup into a lovely tureen and placed it on the waiting trivet. Another large bowl filled with a mixed green salad and a cheese-and-veggie platter were already on the table. I noticed a fruit platter on the counter and Ezekiel bread in the center of the table. Not my preferred bread but the choice of health conscious people. Of whom Hannah was a poster child. And Kaitlin…well, Kaitlin appeared to be evolving into Wannabe Hannah.

Hannah nodded approvingly and filled her bowl with soup. I followed suit and then Kaitlin. The soup was delicious, light and nutritious with cut celery, carrots, and zucchini, and quinoa for extra protein. "I'd love this recipe."

"I'll email it to you," Kaitlin said. "If we had more time, I'd get it now. But I want to bring you up to speed here." She glanced at the clock. "Twenty-one years in forty minutes."

"I'll start," Hannah said. "When we went to high school, Kaitlin and I stayed close, but Sarah went off on her own. She found herself some…uh…different friends."

"Artists, poets, geeks, and loners," Kaitlin explained. "She ended up on the fringes and started behaving oddly. We weren't too surprised when she had her first meltdown in Grade Twelve. She almost lost her year, but admin took pity on her and granted her a diploma after she was released from the hospital. As soon as she graduated, she left Parry Sound and went down south."

"She spent a year living with her older sister in Hamilton, and then she made her way to Toronto," Hannah said. "That was the first step of our grand plan back in Grade Eight. Go to school in Toronto, work for a while, and move to New York."

Kaitlin laughed. "Where I'd be the next Diane Sawyer, Hannah would open a dance school, and Sarah would become a famous fashion designer."

Big city plans for small town girls. At the time, I indulged them and said nothing. I thought their plans far-fetched, but I was prepared to be proven wrong. Of the three, I figured Kaitlin would come the closest to realizing her dream.

"You went to Ryerson," Hannah pointed out. "You could have connected with Sarah."

Another dig at Kaitlin. Was this a regular habit of Hannah's? Did she feel superior because of her better physical image?

Several negative emotions flitted across Kaitlin's face. Pity, regret, shame. She wasn't too comfortable with where the conversation was headed. "I know. I know. But we'd been apart too long. I hadn't contacted her while she was ill, and I felt uncomfortable calling her in Toronto." She raised her eyebrows. "You and Jake were in your own bubble."

Hannah winced, the closest she would get to any negative emotion. Even-keeled to the end, or so she appeared. "I started going steady in Grade Twelve and followed Jake to Western." She blushed and lowered her head. "I took the same courses he did, not even considering what I would like. I was relieved when I got pregnant and didn't have to finish my year."

It would have been the late nineties when Hannah, Kaitlin, and Sarah finished high school. And it sounded like neither woman had made well-thought-out decisions about the future. Following Jake's lead and taking business courses would have been disastrous for Hannah. From what I recalled, she struggled in math and science. She tolerated her courses and looked forward to physical education classes and her dance, gymnastics, and figure skating sessions after school.

While I was interested and wanted to hear more about Kaitlin's and Hannah's trajectories, time was limited. I needed to learn more about Sarah from both women. "What was Sarah doing in Toronto?"

"She started at Humber College but lasted only a year. Afterward, she began her waitressing career." Hannah shook her head. "When I ran into her at Christmas one year, all she could talk about were the great tips she was getting and this fantastic man who was going to marry her and set her up in a condo on the Oakville waterfront."

"That was her longest-lasting relationship," Kaitlin said, rising to remove the tureen and place the fruit platter on the table. "Her mother beamed each time she saw me. She was hoping for an engagement announcement, but it never came."

"We didn't hear anything for the longest time," Hannah said. "I think she might have had another breakdown."

"When did she come here?" I didn't need a play-by-play of Sarah's years in Toronto. It would sadden me even more to hear how dark and desolate those years turned out to be.

"April of this year," Kaitlin said. "She looked great. Pretty, slender, and happy. It was like those bad years never happened."

"Her doctor had finally found the right prescription for her," Hannah said. "For a while, everything seemed to go well. She got a job at a restaurant in Barrie and started teaching yoga part-time on the weekends."

"Did she get training?" Yoga-teacher training was very expensive, but worth it for someone like Sarah who had spiraling moods.

"She was pretty vague about her years in Toronto," Kaitlin said. "But she was good at yoga. You should have…wait, you have a DVD of one of her sessions." She turned toward Hannah.

Hannah frowned. "Somewhere. I'll look for it tonight."

Kaitlin nodded in approval. "You'll see Sarah at her best. Happy and bubbly."

Happy and bubbly were two words I would never have associated with Sarah McHenry. I hoped Hannah would find the DVD. "When did she change?"

Tears brimmed in Kaitlin's eyes. Hannah leaned over to hug her. Both women were quiet for several minutes.

Kaitlin composed herself. "September. She got dark again. She let herself go and gained some weight. The yoga studio laid her off, saying enrollment had dwindled and they would wait until after the fall registration was complete. But we all knew she wouldn't be hired back. Somehow, she managed to keep her job at the restaurant. She…I don't know…" Kaitlin's shoulders drooped.

Hannah grimaced. "That's when she started calling the men. It was so disgusting."

"She called all those men who were at last night's séance," Kaitlin said, her lips tightening. "And she put the moves on Wayne while he was grilling on the deck. I had invited over twenty people to our Labor Day barbecue. She had the nerve to embarrass me in front of my colleagues, Wayne's friends and parents, and my parents. I let her have it and told her I never wanted to see her again."

"Adam tried to downplay it, but I could tell he was uncomfortable with her advances." Hannah lowered her head. "I stopped talking to her as well."

For the month of September, Sarah was alone. Had she picked up her sketch pad and started drawing? Turned to her parents for support? Or had she continued to solicit the attention of men? I suspect it was the latter. A recipe for disaster.

"What do you think happened?" I had to ask the question.

Both girls lowered their heads. They had their suspicions, and I needed to hear them.

Hannah spoke first. "I don't think it was anyone at the séance. I don't see…I can't imagine…" Her voice trailed off.

"I can see one possibility," Kaitlin said, her voice laced with steel, as she turned toward Hannah. "You don't want to see because that would mean accusing part of Dougie's DNA."

Jake Coburn! Kaitlin suspected Jake, and Hannah probably did at some level. I wondered if Cassandra also shared their suspicions. "Why would you say that?"

"We saw the way Jake looked at Sarah when she first arrived." Kaitlin's eyes narrowed. "He flirted with Sarah whenever Cassandra turned her back. And Sarah flirted right back. I don't have any proof, but I think they ended up in bed at some point."

"It could have been just one time," Hannah said.

"That's what you and Cassandra would like to think," Kaitlin said as she shook her head in disapproval.

"Does she know?" I thought back to our dinner last night. I hadn't seen any signs of discontent. If anything, she talked like she was still on her honeymoon.

"She's a psychic," Kaitlin said. "She's got to suspect something. And that's why I think last night's séance was a bust. She heard or sensed something about Jake and freaked out."

"The candles pointed to you," I said.

"Because we know the truth about Jake," Kaitlin said.

Hannah jumped up. "I've got to run. I'm teaching a class in ten minutes."

Kaitlin waited until Hannah's car pulled out of the driveway. She rose and put the cheese platter away. She opened one of the cupboards and took out two loaves wrapped in aluminum foil. She removed the foil and revealed blueberry and banana loaves.

"Time for tea and dessert."

Chapter 16

Kaitlin smiled as she finished eating a generous slice of banana bread. "I need something sweet at lunch. Then I'm okay not having starches and desserts for the rest of the day. Something I've tried to explain to Hannah, who has never had a single craving in her life. It's not natural, not natural at all, to be that disciplined and never let a morsel of dessert cross your lips."

I was also grateful for the sweet bread and cup of echinacea tea. A nice addition to the meal. While I could empathize with Kaitlin, I had to be careful when it came to my own weight. "I love this blueberry bread. So moist. Are these blueberries locally grown?"

Kaitlin nodded. "The girls love blueberry picking. During the summer, we went at least once a week. What we couldn't eat, we froze." Kaitlin rose and put on the kettle to boil more water. "I'm hoping you can stay a bit longer."

I nodded. While several afternoon sessions at the Holistic Fair sounded interesting, there was nothing too new or earth-shattering. I preferred to find out more about Sarah's and Kaitlin's past.

"You've probably figured out that Hannah is still carrying a torch for Jake," Kaitlin said. "She refuses to accept that Jake will never leave Cassandra. It's been over ten years, and Hannah's not getting any younger.

She has to move on."

"She's involved with Adam."

Kaitlin wrinkled her nose. "She's going out with him, but she's not really into him. After the holidays, she'll start taking distance, making excuses about how busy she is with her classes." Kaitlin's eyes flashed in annoyance or perhaps disapproval. "Most of her relationships don't last a year."

I started to comment about Adam's plans for the future and then decided to keep his confidences. Kaitlin and Hannah were still close. I wouldn't want his plans broadcasted. I changed the subject. "So, Jake is the top suspect on your list."

"If we're limiting the suspect pool to everyone who attended last night's séance, I would say yes."

"And if we weren't limiting the suspect pool?"

Kaitlin shrugged. "I'd put my money on someone Sarah picked up at a bar that night. I heard she was drunk, well over the limit. She probably said something inappropriate, or led the man on and proceeded to berate him. She could go hot and cold on people."

A scenario that was beginning to make sense. "Have you shared this with Leo and Cassandra?"

"I did mention it to both of them, but they didn't take it too seriously." Kaitlin chewed her lip, thinking. "I'm not one hundred percent sure, but I think Cassandra talked Leo into having a séance. She's convinced the murderer is one of us."

"Surely, she doesn't suspect you?"

"You heard Bob last night. To most of them, I'm still Meanie, capable of almost anything. Even murder." Tears stung her eyelids.

I leaned over and hugged her. Mean Barbie had

evolved into this strong, sensitive woman who cared about the people in her life. "I don't see you that way."

"But you did back then." Kaitlin smiled as she dabbed at her eyes with a tissue.

"I saw you more like a girl who knew what she wanted and didn't hesitate to ask for it. Not necessarily bad traits."

"I thought I knew what I wanted, but boy, did all that change when I got to Toronto." Kaitlin's eyes brimmed with tears. "I thought everything would work out, but nothing did. I hated the media courses and couldn't stand the competitiveness of the broadcasting industry. I found Toronto too big and impersonal. Believe it or not, I had trouble making friends. The girls were so snippy and competitive. And the boys...well, they only wanted one thing...flings with no strings."

I was surprised to hear Kaitlin had experienced difficulty adapting and making friends. She hadn't given that vibe in Grade Eight. But then she had had Hannah and Sarah as friends to prop her up. Did all mean girls lose confidence when they moved beyond their circle of power?

Kaitlin continued. "At the end of my first year, I switched to general arts and got a degree in English and Psychology. I applied to teacher's college at Nipissing. I missed the North and wanted to get away from southern Ontario. I was able to practice teach here in Parry Sound and accepted the one-year maternity leave when it came up."

"It sounds like you're enjoying teaching."

"I love it, and I'm good at it." Kaitlin blushed. "I know I sound conceited, but it's the truth. At yesterday's conference, I shared some of my teaching strategies and wowed them all. One of the superintendents gave me his card and suggested I contact him when the vice-principal openings for Simcoe County are posted. I'd love to go, but—" Her shoulders slumped.

"You don't want to commute." Having driven that stretch of highway from Barrie to Parry Sound for over two decades, I dreaded the winter driving.

"Not a problem," Kaitlin waved her right hand. "I've got four-wheel drive. And if the roads are bad, I have friends in Orillia and Barrie who would put me up for the night. I don't think Wayne wants me to work outside of Parry Sound. While he's supportive of my career goals, he does want a son. And well, I'd like one too, but I don't want to have to choose between raising a child and advancing in my career."

"You could do both." Not easy, but many of my former colleagues with children were able to balance family life with career advancement.

"I'm tired all the time," Kaitlin confessed. "Adding one more child might do me in."

She did appear more haggard than both Cassandra and Hannah, who were the same age. I squeezed her hand. "If the right job comes up, apply. You may find leadership positions less draining than working in the trenches."

Kaitlin hugged me. "You were my role model, you know. I wasn't just saying that last night. When broadcasting fell through, I thought back to those seven months you spent with us. You made a difference, and I wanted to do the same."

A lump rose in my throat. It had been a while since a student had complimented me. The hug lasted several minutes.

Kaitlin composed herself. "Back to Sarah. I want—and I'm certain we all want—closure. Last night's séance was a bust." She held up her hand. "I know. I know. I was partly to blame. But I couldn't help it. When those two candles pointed in our direction, I lost it."

"What do you think it means?"

Kaitlin lowered her voice. "I suspect Sarah is warning us to be careful."

I tried but couldn't recall Hannah's reaction. Twice, the candles had pointed in her direction, but all she did was gasp. My reaction would have been closer to Kaitlin's. But I knew I had to tread carefully here. I didn't want to cast doubt in Hannah's direction. "How did Hannah feel about the dropped candles?"

"She doesn't set too much store by Cassandra's powers. Considering the past—" Kaitlin paused and averted her glance.

"What about the past?"

"Hannah has never forgiven Cassandra for enticing Jake."

"Enticing is a strange word to be using here."

"Well, Cassandra did inherit a substantial sum after her parents died. And Jake...well, Jake is a lot like his dad. They like money and all the comforts it can buy."

"I'm not following here." I hadn't considered the money angle. From what I could recall, the Coburns were among the wealthiest families in the town. I imagined a healthy trust fund had been set up for both Jake and Adam. Margaret Coburn would have wanted her sons to live comfortable lives.

"Margaret Coburn's family was well-off," Kaitlin

explained. "Hannah told me that Margaret received a sizeable money gift from her parents. Her dowry made it possible for them to live very well in Parry Sound. But Margaret controlled the purse strings. And she wasn't very generous with her husband and sons."

"But Jake was her favorite." The apple of her eye. Whenever the conversation turned to Jake, Margaret's gaze would soften, and her eyes would sparkle. He could do no wrong.

"Margaret wasn't too impressed when he got Hannah pregnant," Kaitlin said as she poured another cup of tea. "She made him promise not to marry Hannah until age twenty-five and then she changed the provisions in the trusts for both sons. Neither one would see a penny until age thirty-five."

"And they knew this?" I could understand her disappointment toward Jake, but I didn't think it appropriate for her to punish Adam as well. And then I recalled his drug and alcohol addiction. Margaret Coburn had chosen to punish both sons for their early transgressions. I wondered how she had punished her husband.

"Jake was furious, but he had to hold in all that rage. Margaret was in the final stages of ovarian cancer and dying."

I wondered about Adam's reaction. Had he confronted his mother or chosen to stay quiet? While I suspected the latter, I could be wrong. Having to delay access to a large chunk of cash could upset almost anyone's apple cart. My thoughts turned to Jake. Had he decided on Plan B and pursued Cassandra instead?

"Hannah and I often wonder if Cassandra ever figured it out," Kaitlin said as she stirred her tea. "After the Maddalones died, Cassandra's brother, Lorenzo, turned to Mr. Coburn for advice about his parents' estate. Mr. Coburn must have shared the news with Jake, who had started to work in the accounting office."

How much money did they leave her? Had Cassandra turned over the management of the estate to Jake? I felt sick to my stomach at the thought of all this deception. I recalled what Kaitlin had said about the trusts. All my students had turned thirty-five this past year. "Adam and Jake must have tapped into their trusts."

Kaitlin shook her head. "They're New Year's babies. They won't be able to access the money until January."

Another sizeable chunk of money. I was happy to hear Adam would be getting his share. As for Jake, I wondered what he would do. Would he leave Cassandra?

Kaitlin smiled tightly. "Jake won't leave Cassandra. It's too comfortable for him. The occasional fling doesn't mean anything to him. He's his father's son."

"Excuse me?"

"Oh, Gilda! Don't tell me you didn't know about Mr. Coburn's roving eyes and hands. He's always liked the ladies. And the ladies liked him right back. He was, and still is, the ultimate man whore."

"Kaitlin!"

"It's true. He sponged off Margaret and—" The landline rang. Kaitlin frowned at the call display and picked up the receiver. She lowered her voice. "Hi, Ann. How are you doing?"

Kaitlin said nothing for a while, but I could feel her

gaze upon me. "She's here right now. I'll let you speak to her." She cupped the receiver. "It's Ann McHenry. Sarah's mom."

I took the phone. "Hello, Mrs. McHenry. I was so sorry to hear about Sarah. My condolences to you and your family."

"Thank you, Gilda." She paused. "Please call me Ann. I was wondering if you could drop by this afternoon."

It was getting close to one-thirty. Still early. I didn't have to be at Vera's until five o'clock. As for the Holistic Fair, I had planned to return but could pass on the sessions and exhibits. "I can come over now."

Chapter 17

While driving to see Mrs. McHenry, I reviewed all that Kaitlin and Hannah had shared. It seemed money—or lack of it—was at the base of almost every decision made for the past two decades. Had Margaret Coburn chosen to leave the trusts alone, Jake might have married Hannah. Or not. I still maintained he had a soft spot for Cassandra that had been evident during their Grade Eight year. He might have considered pursuing her but didn't want to deal with her strict parents. And the Barbies were enticing. All of them bursting with blonde loveliness. Thinking back, I recall Jake being very much taken by all three of them. He ended up with Kaitlin because of her aggressiveness at the time.

His philandering disturbed me. Did he indulge in flings or longer relationships? Neither was good, but I felt more at ease believing he wouldn't enter into a long-term relationship with anyone other than Cassandra. As for Cassandra not knowing, I had to agree with Kaitlin. With those heightened intuitive powers, how could she miss the signs? Not even a man-whore-in-training would be capable of maintaining a long-term deception.

Man whore. Douglas Coburn. Those images didn't connect. While there had been staff room discussion about all the fathers, I hadn't paid any attention to it. Still in recovery from my disastrous marriage, I had no desire to connect with another man. I had only one date during my seven months in Parry Sound.

Leo Mulligan. He hadn't come up at all in the conversation. Only one mention about Kaitlin sharing her opinion about the possible murderer. Part of me wanted to believe Kaitlin. How much safer to think an outsider had taken advantage of Sarah and not someone who had known her since kindergarten.

My thoughts gravitated toward Hannah. Something didn't ring true there. She appeared so calm, so collected. And convinced Jake couldn't have harmed Sarah. But she didn't offer any theories. None at all. That puzzled me. A disturbing thought entered my consciousness. Could Hannah and Sarah have had an altercation that ended in a tragic accident?

While Kaitlin reacted swiftly to Sarah's advances toward Wayne, Hannah appeared to have a more subdued reaction to Sarah's overtures toward Adam. Last night, I gathered she wasn't into him, but I don't think she would have appreciated Sarah or any other woman pursuing her man.

Would Hannah leave Adam after Christmas—right before he received his trust fund? I wondered about the amount of the trust and if it would be enough to entice Hannah, who had always been a high-maintenance girl. In Grade Eight, she had been the first to sport the latest fashion trend. The youngest and a daddy's girl, she could wrap her father around her finger and persuade him to drive down to Toronto for a day of shopping. Her more practical mother rolled her eyes but said nothing.

As I pulled into the McHenry driveway, I took several deep breaths. I had only one recollection of

Mrs. McHenry, a quiet woman who said very little during our short interview on Parents' Night. She had come alone. Not too uncommon, but I did wonder about Mr. McHenry. I recalled Sarah groaning whenever his name came up, but that was common among adolescent girls.

Mrs. McHenry opened the door within seconds of my knocks. She embraced me and led me into a small parlor. Everything shone, but there was a dejected air of sadness. I suspect Mrs. McHenry buried her feelings by cleaning and decluttering.

She motioned toward the love seat and sat in the large armchair across from me. "Can I get you something—tea, coffee?"

I held up my hand. "I'm stuffed. I had lunch at Kaitlin's."

Mrs. McHenry sighed. "I remember when the three of them would spend entire days together. When Sarah returned in April, I thought they would connect again." She paused. "They did for a while."

How much did she know of Sarah's overtures toward other men? Would Leo have informed or spared her? I could state arguments for both sides.

Mrs. McHenry smiled, a tentative smile that livened up her features. "I was happy to hear you'd come back to help…help…" Her hand shook.

I leaned over and squeezed her hand. "I'm so sorry. I hope we can find out who hurt Sarah."

"I'd like that as well," she said, speaking very slowly. "But Stuart…my husband isn't too happy with opening up this investigation. I hate to say it, but I think he was more comfortable when everyone thought Sarah had harmed herself." A sob escaped, and she cried softly.

"I could never think that." In spite of her mercurial moods in school, I didn't think Sarah capable of killing herself. Her artwork was always filled with light and fluffy images. And during the spring when she worked on the yearbook, I couldn't recall a single dark period.

"You were so wonderful to her. When you appointed her co-editor of the yearbook, she came home practically walking on air. She and Adam went steady for a while. I know they were young, but I hoped they would continue once they got into high school. They were so much alike, and I thought he was the nicer brother. I don't put too much store in looks and superficial charm."

"Neither do I," I found myself agreeing. Adam remained my favorite of the two Coburn brothers. And I did agree that he and Sarah would have been well-matched. But Adam was besotted with Hannah. I doubt he even gave Sarah a second glance.

Mrs. McHenry picked up a burgundy-covered book. The yearbook. "I found this book while I was cleaning out Sarah's room…right after they found her body. I decided not to share with Stuart or the police. I hid the book and, well…I was going to keep it for myself. But I thought you might want it."

"I have my own copy. Why don't you keep it?"

She shook her head. "There are some papers in there you might be able to figure out."

"Papers?" Had Sarah kept copies of old layouts?

"Her poems."

"Sarah wrote poetry?" I remembered spending some time discussing poetry during the English classes, but none of the students had shown any interest. They had all complained when I assigned creative poetry exercises.

Mrs. McHenry shrugged. "It's not the kind of poetry I learned in school. Very little rhymes and everything's all over the place, but you might be able to figure it out." She shuddered. "I think she wrote some of those poems during those last weeks."

Had Sarah left clues? I felt uneasy about trying to parse her work. "Maybe you should give the papers to Leo Mulligan."

"I don't trust him," Mrs. McHenry said, her eyes narrowing into slits.

"Pardon?"

"When he's on the prowl, no woman is safe, especially if she's young, pretty, and blonde."

I felt a pang of disappointment. I hadn't gotten that vibe from Leo. In fact, I picked up on his attraction to me. And I'm neither young nor blonde. As for pretty, I do get my share of compliments, but I couldn't compete with women fifteen years younger.

Mrs. McHenry shook her head. "I thought you'd see beyond his charms. But I guess you're like the rest of them."

I chose to ignore the innuendo. "Did he pursue Sarah?"

"He came by a couple of times and took her out, and then he stopped." Mrs. McHenry's lips tightened. "She started going with someone else. I'm not certain who, but I think he might be a married man. It fell apart sometime toward the end of August. That's when she started drinking and spending more time alone in her room."

Jake Coburn came to mind. Possibly Bob, Daniel,

or Adam. The last three were long-shots. I couldn't imagine Bob or Daniel cheating on their wives. As for Adam, he didn't seem to be the two-timing type. All the signs pointed to Jake.

I opened the yearbook to the loose pages. All handwritten with different colors of ink. Some pages were more worn than others, but the handwriting appeared consistent. Surprising there were no significant changes over the years. My handwriting had deteriorated with the advent of computers. During the last ten years of teaching, I had to print on the blackboards.

Several phrases caught my attention:

"Longing to see you once more…"

"Languishing without your touch…"

"Your hot breath caressing my face…"

As I flipped through the pages, I wondered about the order. She had not dated her poems. I would have to read them and try to come up with the most likely sequence. Right now, I needed to focus on Mrs. McHenry, who wore an air of expectancy. While I couldn't bring back Sarah, I could help find the person who had harmed her. "What do you think happened?"

She averted her face and tried to compose her features. She took a deep breath and said, "Each day, I think something different happened. I know who they suspect but I…I…"

"Who do they suspect?"

Her voice was resigned. "One of those four men."

"Jake, Adam, Bob, and Daniel?" I left out Leo and wondered if she would comment on the probability of him harming Sarah. Something I found far-fetched, but maybe I needed to consider all possibilities.

She nodded. "I've known their mothers for decades. We met for coffee and played bridge. I…I find it hard to believe one of their sons hurt Sarah."

I found it difficult to imagine Margaret Coburn and Ann McHenry as friends. But stranger alliances have been formed. In spite of her haughty air, Margaret must have realized she needed to connect with the mothers of her sons' playmates. It would not have made sense to isolate her sons.

Mrs. McHenry continued. "I think Sarah connected with a married man and starting making unrealistic demands. The man lost patience and shoved her. I don't think he meant to kill her, but he did. And then he panicked and ran."

Kaitlin's theory, as well. And to be truthful, it did make sense. If Sarah hadn't sent the email to me, I imagine Leo would have also accepted that theory. I reminded Mrs. McHenry of the email.

She shook her head. "I don't know what she meant by it. She could have been having one of her blue days and thinking of how everyone had abandoned her." Her eyes brimmed with tears. "I wasn't too surprised about Kaitlin. She had a habit of freezing out her friends. Hannah disappointed me."

Had Hannah abandoned Sarah after she propositioned their men? Did Mrs. McHenry not know all the details? I kept my silence. There was no point adding to her pain and suffering.

"If Eileen lived closer, she could have visited more often." Mrs. McHenry said, as she struggled to keep the tears from forming.

Eileen? And then I recalled that Sarah had a sister in southern Ontario and a brother somewhere out west.

The door opened, and a gust of cold air blew in. Mrs. McHenry grabbed the yearbook and thrust it into my tote. It was taller than my tote, but not noticeably so. She straightened her hair and forced a smile as she glanced beyond me. "Gilda Battista…Sarah's Grade Eight teacher dropped by." She paused. "Gilda, this is my husband Stuart."

I turned and met the gaze of a much older man. Sporting longish gray hair under a Labatt's Blue cap and stooped in his posture, he appeared at least two decades older than his wife. And he looked annoyed. Did he resent the fact that I was a visitor or the reference to Sarah?

He nodded in my direction and grunted. "Ma'am." He turned to his wife. "Ted Mason said he'd drop by and take a look at the sink in the basement. No point paying a plumber if it's not necessary. I'll wait for him downstairs." Before she could answer, he left the room. A tightness spread over Mrs. McHenry's features, signaling the visit was over.

Having met Stuart McHenry for the first time, I didn't know if he had always been this sullen or if time and circumstances had altered him. It would have been very difficult to watch Sarah experience meltdowns during her teens and bear witness as she succumbed to the disease again and again. Sarah might have reached out for help during those dark years after her southern Ontario benefactor left her. Mrs. McHenry would have responded, but Mr. McHenry would have taken distance and eventually lost patience.

I leaned over and whispered, "I'll read the poems."

She squeezed my hand. "Thank you, Gilda. I'll call if I remember anything else."

Chapter 18

Two thirty. Still early enough, but I had no intention of returning to the Holistic Fair. I would be too distracted to attend any of the lectures, and I had no desire to visit the psychics or any of the other booths. Maria and Rosa would fill me in on their adventures later in the afternoon.

As I drove to the hotel, I reviewed my conversation with Mrs. McHenry. While she claimed not to understand Sarah's poetry, she might have seen something she wanted me to notice and act upon. Possibly a reference to a classmate or a male character trait I would recognize. Thinking back, all I could recall was that the Barbies, Cassandra, and all the other girls in the class had crushes on Jake. They tried to pretend otherwise, but it never worked. Whenever Jake asked a question or left his desk, seven sets of eyes would turn in his direction. I tried but couldn't recall any of the other nine boys generating that level of interest. Unless, of course, the boy got into trouble and then all eyes would turn in his direction.

Bob and Daniel. While Bob's nickname was Clearasil, I couldn't recall Daniel's. And I couldn't recall a single incident where Daniel captured my attention. He was one of those quiet, well-behaved students who are forgotten as soon as they leave the classroom. Often, those students go on and outperform their more extroverted counterparts. At some point this evening, I would ask Daniel and Bob to tell me more about their computer leasing business.

I pulled into the parking lot and made my way to my hotel room. I took off my jacket and made myself comfortable in one of the large armchairs. I read each poem twice, deciding whether or not it was relevant to the present. It wasn't hard to figure out which poems were written during Sarah's teens. While the handwriting hadn't changed significantly, the word usage and quality of the paper had evolved. In her teens, Sarah used loose-leaf and foolscap. Also, there was more rhyme and contrived structures in the adolescent poetry. The later poems were all written in free verse on stationery paper.

I sorted the poems into two piles: Review and Discard. I ended up with nine poems requiring closer attention. I smiled at the three odes from Grade Eight: "Ode to Adam," "Ode to Barbies," "Ode to Ms. B." We had studied the "Ode to Ozymandias," and I had assigned an exercise where the students had to write an ode to their favorite person or thing. To my surprise, everyone liked the idea of writing poetry that wasn't constrained by fixed stanza length or rhyme scheme.

While I couldn't recall which of the odes Sarah had submitted, I doubt it was the "Ode to Ms. B." I would have made a copy and kept it in my files. During my teaching years, I saved all the cards and notes I received from students, parents, and administrators. I don't recall ever seeing this particular ode.

I teared up as I reread those last three lines:

Thank you for being our friend
Holding our hands and our hearts

And taking us to the end.

The last week in June had been an emotional time for all of us. The students hated to see me leave Parry Sound and pursue teaching jobs in southern Ontario. I had been offered a permanent contract, but I couldn't see myself staying in such a small community. Nor could I return to Sudbury for weekends or longer periods. I had started to recover from Luigi's betrayal, but I couldn't deal with running into him or anyone who knew of the circumstances that had ended our marriage. I had hoped to keep the details private, but Luigi didn't help matters when he turned up everywhere in Sudbury with his partner in tow.

I forced myself to focus on the next poem: "Ode to Barbies."

The poem confirmed what I already knew. Kaitlin was the ringleader and the other two followers. In the poem and in several of our private conversations, Sarah chafed at the constraints of their friendship but didn't want to break up with them. She did take some distance when Adam came into the picture. From the conversation with Kaitlin and Hannah, I gathered Sarah had purposely sought out different friends in high school.

I smiled at the "Ode to Adam."

A sweet poem! The kind a young girl would put in a Valentine or birthday card. Tempted to show it to Adam, I dismissed the thought. It would sadden him, and he might tell Hannah, who hadn't been too thrilled when Sarah propositioned him. But if Hannah were planning to end the relationship after the holidays, would she be too upset if Adam moved on first?

The remaining six poems had been written

recently. No rhyming, and jumbled-up phrases and references that could mean almost anything. Was she referring to her former classmates or other men she had met?

A Cautionary Tale
What will they say
when I return
with my tail between my legs?
No job
No money
No man
They'll cross the street,
averting their glances
As the spring breeze
carries their whispers
She's the cautionary tale
The one you don't want to be.

I had winced when Cassandra referred to Sarah as a cautionary table. I was even more distressed to hear Sarah classify herself as one. This poem must have been written as she contemplated returning to Parry Sound. Deciding to return home after spending years away is not an easy decision. Especially when those years away did not yield a livelihood or husband. While I didn't know all the particulars of Sarah's life, I didn't imagine she would have had a healthy nest egg. And from what Kaitlin and Hannah had shared, Sarah didn't have a man in her life when she arrived in April.

Homecoming
All gussied up
Toned and tanned to perfection!
Fresh blond highlights and layers of makeup
Smoke and mirrors

I can do that so well
And fool everybody
Even the Barbies
Who once knew all the tricks
Have they forgotten?
I haven't
And that's why I'll get
Who they have
And who they want to have.

A definite change of mood. I wondered how much time had elapsed between the two poems. It could have been days or even weeks. People who suffered from the bipolar disorder were easily triggered. I recalled several colleagues and students who appeared perfectly fine one day and were suddenly on sick leave the following day. At least, they had appeared fine. But then, I hadn't been close enough to notice anything off or out of the ordinary. I imagined family members would have no problems identifying potential triggers.

From the last three lines, it was very clear Sarah was eyeing Wayne Grant and Adam Coburn. But that could have been just the beginning. Sarah appeared determined to outshine and outdo Kaitlin and Hannah. So much unfinished business from the past. That last line—*And who they want to have*—could only refer to one person: Jake Coburn. Interestingly enough, there was no mention of Cassandra. Had Sarah dismissed her as a rival? Had Cassandra picked up on Sarah's interest in Jake? Again, I wondered about the reliability of her psychic abilities.

Not for Me
Definitely a start
One that seems to please

And relieve
All who are watching
Or pretending not to watch.
It would be so easy
Oh so easy
To fall under the spell
Of eyes as dark as midnight
And broad shoulders
Accustomed to heavy lifting.
Too safe
Too predictable
And Not For Me!

One phrase stuck out: *Eyes as dark as midnight.* This had to be Leo. While I wasn't one hundred percent certain, I doubted there were too many other men in Parry Sound with such distinctive eyes. Maria and Rosa had commented on them. I was certain other women took notice of those mesmerizing eyes that seemed to see all and know all. I didn't recall noticing his eyes twenty-one years ago. Back then, he had those Black Irish looks. The blue-black hair had complemented the eyes, while today's white hair accentuated them.

Ann and Stuart McHenry had approved of Leo Mulligan. An older, well-established man would provide stability and respectability for their wayward daughter. But the age difference was too much for Sarah. And so she left him. I wondered if Sarah shared her misgivings with anyone. Ann had mentioned a sister. Had the two siblings been close? So many questions arose as I read these poems. Questions that only someone close to Sarah could answer.

A Blast from the Past
I had hoped to hear back

To see what could happen
If sparks could still fly
And evolve
Into something more lasting
More satisfying.
Our bodies remembered
and rekindled that flame.
I'm longing to see you once more
And feel your hot breath
caressing my face.
Whenever we're apart
I find myself
languishing without your touch.
But will it last?
Will it extinguish
The competing flame
Or will it slowly die out
Leaving me alone once more?

A Blast from the past. Definitely more telling. She
had hooked up with someone from her early years in
Parry Sound. While my thoughts immediately
gravitated toward elementary school, it could have been
someone from high school. One of the poets, artists, or
loners she had hung around with. The details were too
sketchy, and the references to their love-making
generic.

The competing flame. The man was married or
involved with another woman. Jake. Adam. Daniel.
Bob. All four fit that criterion. And I imagine the other
men also had women in their lives.

Shattered
You hurled your words
Like well-sharpened arrows

And found an easy mark
One much too close
To the broken heart
That has shattered once more.
You don't care
You don't even want to care
I can hear it in your voice
A profound relief
A gurgling happiness.
A convenient loss
That pleases you so much.

Had she been pregnant? Had a miscarriage or abortion? And had the man walked away, relieved and happy to be rid of Sarah?

"*A convenient loss*
That pleases you so much."

Mrs. McHenry might have also picked up on this revelation. I tried to recall the timeline Kaitlin and Hannah had provided. Sarah had appeared heavy and unhappy during Labor Day weekend. She could have been pregnant at the time or recovering from a miscarriage or abortion.

According to Mrs. McHenry, her mood plummeted in mid-August. It could have been when she lost the child or when the man distanced himself. Not too many married men would want to stick around when their girlfriends got pregnant and started talking about their future lives together.

Alone
What is the point…
Of going on
Trying once more
To find my place in the sun.

Only clouds appear
Dark, ominous clouds
And torrential rains drown out my dreams
The men come and go
Taking what they need
And taking their leave
With no thought to me or my feelings.
I'm an empty shell
With no love and no hope.
A discarded woman
Who'll always be alone.

This was the last poem Sarah wrote. Dark from start to finish with no glimmers of hope. The dream man could be almost anyone: a former classmate or an acquaintance from long ago. Whoever he was, he had done a number on Sarah. Lost and bereft, she must have searched for a confidant and then sent the infamous email to me. In spite of what Carlo had said, I felt some responsibility for her death. I could have listened and provided some clarity. I could have... I could have invited her to visit me in Sudbury and get away from whatever and whoever was disturbing her.

Chapter 19

Quarter to four. I had spent over two hours reading and analyzing Sarah's poems. I would put them aside and reread them later, before going to bed. I was hoping a comment or action at tonight's séance would trigger a revelation.

As I started to put the yearbook away, I noticed a yellow post-it note sticking out from one of the pages. Had Sarah or Mrs. McHenry marked that page? I followed the note and opened the book to the Autograph section. During my teaching years, I would sign yearbooks but avert my eyes from the other messages that often contained suggestive and colorful language. But today, I needed to read all the student messages.

Scanning the two pages, I could easily pick out the female autographs: rounded letters with hearts and flourishes, often written using pink or purple markers. I saw three different comments from Kaitlin and two from Hannah, all of them hinting at a fabulous future in Toronto and New York City. The other girls in the class wrote short congratulatory messages, wishing Sarah luck in the future.

Most of the boys—including Bob and Daniel— signed their names. Jake added, "See you around, kid." Two messages from Adam mentioned their time on the yearbook and plans to get together in the summer.

Rereading the messages, I was gratified to see no swear words or inappropriate comments. Scanning the page one last time, I noticed the small black arrow at the bottom of the second page pointing to the right. I turned the page and gasped at the large graphic and bold, calligraphic letters enclosed in a box. Two connecting hearts in red appeared in the middle of the box. Above the hearts, appeared *To: See-Ker-256* on the first line followed by *From: See-Ker-789*, both in black, block letters. Below the heart, Forever and a Day appeared in large calligraphic letters.

Goose bumps rose on my arms. I flipped back to the previous pages and checked each of the male entries. All ten boys had commented at least once, Adam twice. Logic would point to Adam, who had been close to Sarah throughout the winter and spring. But why use codes?

I could spend the rest of the day pondering this dilemma. But I had a dinner invitation I couldn't cancel. I would read the poems later. Or maybe that wouldn't be necessary. If all went well at tonight's séance, the mystery man would be revealed.

Chapter 20

I would have to scramble if I wanted to arrive at Vera's before five o'clock. Knowing Vera, dinner would be on time. When it came to mealtimes, Italian women of that generation held fast to either five o'clock or five-thirty, whatever time their husbands had preferred during their working years. In my mother's house, five-thirty was the golden time. Occasionally six o'clock, but never later.

I rummaged through my duffle bag for something to wear other than my jeans and sweats. I settled on black pants, a royal blue blouse, and a black vest. Hopefully, not too dressy for the séance afterward. I freshened my makeup and left. I picked up a bottle of wine and arrived at Vera's by ten to five. Cutting it close, but still in time to chat for a short while.

I had no problems finding the house. From the exterior, very little appeared to have changed in the past two decades. In spite of their challenges, the Lodestros—like all other Italian immigrants—believed in the importance of curb appeal long before the home stagers coined the expression. *Bella veduta.* Whatever the circumstances, make a good impression with your appearance, your house, and your life.

As soon as Vera opened the door, she engulfed me in a tight hug. After we separated, I stood back and admired the septuagenarian who could pass for a woman in her early sixties. Her short hair was a dark, auburn color and her eyes sparkled with mischief. Was that eyeliner and mascara? She wore jeans, dark blue wash, with a loose, gypsy top and silver jewelry. The Vera I once knew had lived in baggy housedresses and barely had time to comb her hair. As for make-up, I don't recall ever seeing her wear it. This new incarnation seemed to have shed her old persona, along with thirty pounds. Size ten, maybe even size eight.

"Doesn't she look like a teenager?" Maria said, as she approached and gave me another hug.

"And acts like one," Rosa said, crushing me with a third hug. "She's even got a boyfriend."

We all laughed. I entered and glanced around the room, hoping to meet Vera's friend. I always hated it when people referred to Carlo as my boyfriend. "Boy" sounds so juvenile, especially if the man is over thirty. Partner and man friend sound just as awkward. As for Vera's friend, he would be over seventy. Or maybe not. The new Vera could slip into a cougar role.

Vera shook her head. "He has his place. I have mine. We don't spend every minute together."

More laughter as I followed Vera into the living area. The interior of her house had also undergone a makeover. While I couldn't recall too many details from two decades ago, I knew she didn't have a white sofa, glass coffee table with a ceramic bottom, or delicate lamps. An impossibility with five rambunctious children, a husband, and a mother-in-law all crammed into the small house. But it didn't appear small tonight. Instead, spacious came to mind.

"Your house looks beautiful," I said. "Did you hire a designer?"

Vera shrugged. "Sandra took care of it." Sandra, not Cassandra. I imagined it would be difficult for a close relative to shift gears.

Before Vera could clarify, the phone rang. Vera shook her head and laughed as she picked up her smart phone. Another change, one my mother, Maria, and Rosa would never consider. "What's wrong?" She listened for a while and moved the phone away but close enough for the other person to hear. "My Barrie daughter forgot to check the freezer before promising everyone pasta with pesto. And now, she has to make the pesto herself." She spoke into the phone. "Give me a minute. I'll have to find the recipe." She turned back to us. "It has to be precise for Angela."

She walked toward the kitchen and closed the door behind her.

Maria leaned over and whispered, "When Sandra got her inheritance, she paid off Vera's mortgage and gave her one hundred thousand dollars."

A princely sum at any time. And twenty years ago, that sum would have gone even farther, especially with people as frugal as Vera and Dario Lodestro. Dear Dario. Such a kind, thoughtful man, who never raised his voice. His children adored him and would clamor around his legs whenever he came back from work. He was always happy to see me at the dinner table and each time would repeat his offer to help in any way. I recalled sending a condolence card a while back, maybe five or six years ago. Had it been that long?

I glanced at the kitchen door and then turned to Maria and Rosa. "What else do you know?" I couldn't ask such an open-ended question of too many people. But with Maria and Rosa, there would be no judgment.

"The inheritance was big...over a million dollars," Maria said.

"The husband is getting almost two million of his own after Christmas," Rosa added.

Tidy sums, indeed! I wondered if Hannah knew how much Adam would be worth. And if she did, would her attitude change? Living in her parents' house was comfortable, but she could live so much better and even leave Parry Sound.

I felt happy for Adam, who deserved a break, one delayed unnecessarily in my opinion. Margaret Coburn behaved much too cruelly. I suspect she was more disappointed with the man whore she had married, and believed that by punishing his sons, she would also be punishing him. I hoped Adam would budget his money and not indulge in any wild shopping sprees.

Maria started to speak but stopped when the kitchen door opened. Vera chuckled. "I've told Angela millions of time. Plan ahead. Don't wait until the last minute before checking the freezer. I left her five jars of pesto when I visited last month."

I also loved pesto and often used it when I cooked my salmon. Five jars wouldn't last too long in my kitchen.

"It's easy enough to make," Maria said. "And you gave her the recipe."

"Which she already had somewhere in that kitchen of hers," Vera said and then waved her hand. "But enough about Angela's disorganized life." Vera turned to me. "I hear you've become an ambulance chaser in Sudbury. And now you've decided to add Parry Sound to your list."

Maria and Rosa must have spent the entire

afternoon updating Vera. I wondered how much Cassandra had shared with her aunt. Did Vera know about the missed email? I decided not to mention it. "When Leo called, I felt I had to come and try to help."

"Leo?" Maria asked as she exchanged glances with Rosa.

"The wolf," Vera said, hiding a smile. "He can be very persuasive."

Maria's eyes bulged. "He's trouble."

"Lots of it," Rosa said. She pointed to me. "Gilda's got a man already. A good one."

"Ah yes, the Chief Detective," Vera said, winking in my direction."It's too bad he couldn't accompany you."

No secrets here! All was on the table, ready to be analyzed and dissected. I would get many earfuls tonight.

"When is he coming home?" Maria asked. "It's been over two weeks."

"Soon," I said. At least, I hoped it would be sometime this week. He had about five weeks of accumulated vacation time that we had planned to use when we went on safari to South Africa. But I hesitated to remind Carlo of those tentative plans. He was enjoying his time out west, especially the family reunions.

"Hmm." Rosa shook her head. "Does he know you're here?"

"Yes," I said, thinking about the phone call that would come later in the evening. Hopefully, tonight's séance would bring closure, and I would have good news to report.

"He's helping his daughter and grandsons get

settled in Vancouver," Maria explained. "Tania, the daughter, has to live near the toad. It's the law."

I smiled at the mention of the toad. In the six months that Maria, Rosa, and my mother had befriended Tania, they had heard all the details of the toad's betrayal. While Tania and I were on speaking terms, there wasn't too much warmth there. For Carlo's sake, we tolerated each other.

Maria and Rosa exchanged glances. I imagined they wanted to add their own spin on my relationship with Carlo. Normally, I would move on and change the subject, but I suddenly felt the need to unburden myself. "He's thinking of moving out there."

Maria's eyebrows jumped while Rosa's mouth formed a small o.

"Is Tania his only child?" Vera asked, giving me her full attention.

"No, he has a son, Steve, who lives in Calgary." I paused and added, "A short plane ride to Vancouver."

Vera digested this information and then spoke slowly. "I'd want to move out there as well. I couldn't bear to be too far from my children. As it is now, I'm not too happy with the two who are living in Windsor and Hamilton."

"Gilda doesn't have any sisters or brothers," Maria said. "She'd be leaving her mother alone in Sudbury."

"Assunta leaves Gilda alone for six months of the year," Vera said, turning in my direction. "You could compromise and spend half the year in Sudbury and the other half in Vancouver. Go there when your mother goes to Italy."

An awkward silence followed and then Vera pointed toward a room to her left. "Let's eat."

Chapter 21

We followed Vera to a spacious room with a light oak table and matching chairs. A large buffet dominated one wall and groupings of family pictures took care of the remaining walls. I couldn't recall ever eating in this room, and I had shared several meals with Vera and her brood.

Vera smiled at my confusion. "This was the girls' bedroom. As soon as my youngest left home, I converted it into a dining room." She pointed to the head of the table. "Your place, Gilda." Whenever I had visited, she waved me to the head of the table, an honor in an Italian household.

Maria and Rosa sat across from each other. Vera went back into the kitchen and brought out the salads. To my surprise, I was hungry and found myself eating quickly. I clapped with delight when I saw the next course: stuffed pasta shells. Vera, like my mother, remembered everyone's favorite dishes. Maria and Rosa nodded approvingly.

An animated discussion followed, comparing different peeled tomatoes and pastas on the market. I never noticed the difference among the various brands of pasta or tomatoes. But the foodies of the world did. Again, I wondered how the foodie gene could have bypassed me. It seemed everyone in my circle, Italians and non-Italians, had some level of foodiness. Was there even such a word? I would have to Google it later.

Dessert was fruit and frozen yogurt. A change from the rich desserts of the past, and I suspect there must have been an animated discussion during the afternoon. Maria and Rosa could have whipped up one of their signature desserts, but I imagine Vera had won that battle. It was her kitchen, and she was in charge.

While we were having our coffees, Maria brought up the murder. "Who do you think did it?"

While I had considered several scenarios, I wasn't prepared to share any of them with these well-meaning but chatty ladies. I shrugged. "I can't imagine any of the students killing Sarah. They're good kids."

"Good kids don't always grow up into good adults," Vera said, as she stirred her coffee. "Twenty-one years is a long time, and bad things can happen to good people."

I nodded, thinking of all the tragedy that had surrounded my young students.

First and foremost, the death of the elder Maddalones, an accident that had changed the trajectory of Cassandra's life. Margaret Coburn's cancer diagnosis and subsequent death also affected her sons. Jake had turned to Hannah for comfort, while Adam had sought solace in drugs and alcohol. Had Margaret been healthy, she would have maintained a tighter rein on both her sons and possibly averted the unexpected pregnancy and addiction problems.

In fact, everyone's life trajectory would have been altered by the presence of a healthy Margaret Coburn. Dougie might not have been conceived, Jake may have stayed a bachelor longer, and Cassandra might have left Parry Sound and started over elsewhere.

Sarah McHenry was the only one unaffected by Margaret's death. Her meltdowns and relationships—or more accurately flings—were of her own doing. Not to blame Sarah or her parents, but an intervention could have made a positive difference.

"It has to be one of the boys...men," Rosa said.

Vera nodded. "Sarah drank and fooled around too much. She was a pretty girl, but not too many men would put up with her behavior."

Maria turned toward me. "Was she like that in school?"

"She kept to herself." Like all the other girls, she had a crush on Jake, but she never acted upon it. If I had to say which Barbie I would have considered most likely to become wild and promiscuous, I would point to Kaitlin.

"You have to watch the quiet ones," Rosa said. "You never know what they're thinking."

"I've known those kids and their parents all their lives," Vera said, speaking slowly. "Everyone did their best to raise them properly, but mental illness throws a monkey wrench into everything." She shook her head. "Poor Adam. He was so smart in school, and he got all those scholarships. Who would have thought he'd have trouble hanging onto a job and end up in rehab three times."

I hoped Adam would visit me in Sudbury. When I extended the invitation, I hadn't known about the trusts. But even with a nice cushion, Adam needed help figuring out what he wanted to do with his life. In my opinion, he should not remain in Parry Sound. Nor should he marry his brother's ex-girlfriend and help raise his brother's son. But if Kaitlin was right, Hannah would end everything right after Christmas. A blessing in disguise though Adam might think differently.

"Who's Adam?" Maria asked.

I let Vera answer. She gave a summary of Adam's early life and present situation. From her tone, I suspected she also had a soft spot for Adam. I wondered what she thought of Jake but felt awkward bringing up his name. I didn't want her to think I suspected Jake. Which in truth I was starting to do. Jake and Leo. Top suspects in the séance pool.

Both Maria and Rosa held up their fingers in the L-salute. Vera frowned. I explained how one of Maria's grandsons had shared the "Loser" salute with his grandmother and great-aunt who then passed it on to my mother and other friends.

Vera laughed as she fiddled with her fingers. "I'll have to remember the salute. But I don't want to use it with Adam. He's too nice."

"Let's hope your niece can figure everything out tonight," Rosa said. "We have to leave tomorrow morning. My new grandson—Richard—is having his christening at the eleven o'clock Mass. I don't want to be late."

Maria rolled her eyes in my direction. "It won't be a problem. If we leave at eight o'clock, we'll get to Sudbury by nine-thirty."

"I would have liked to have gotten my hair done before the Mass," Rosa said. "They'll be taking pictures."

Vera reached for her smart phone. "I can get you appointments tomorrow morning. The woman three doors down is a retired hairdresser. She's up at five o'clock every morning."

Rosa clapped her hands and Maria nodded. Vera punched in a code, spoke to the woman, and made appointments for seven o'clock and seven-thirty.

"You handle that phone like the young kids," Maria said with a wistful tone. "You've kept up."

"I've had to," Vera said. "If I want to communicate with my grandchildren, I have to text and go on Facebook."

Maria's eyes popped. To her, Facebook was an unfathomable black hole she feared and resented. She depended upon Belinda for Facebook updates and help with her antiquated cell phone. Rosa didn't own a cell phone and had no interest in going online.

Vera rose. "I'll make a fresh pot of coffee." She smiled at me. "You have time for one last cup before you have to go."

Maria and Rosa waited for Vera to leave the room.

"She's changed a lot," Maria said, twinges of envy in her voice.

"It must be all the sex she's having," Rosa said.

"Rosa!" Both Maria and I spoke at the same time. Rosa hadn't whispered, and I feared Vera would overhear.

Rosa shrugged. "It's the only explanation I can come up with. We saw her two years ago, and she was still mourning Dario. She's changed since meeting that man."

"Who is he?" I was curious about the man who had brought about this amazing transformation.

"A widower from Nova Scotia," Maria said. "He's Canadian. That's all she said." Vera had managed to maintain a modicum of privacy. Not easy to do with Maria and Rosa, who picked up on every nuance in conversation and gesture.

"I think he's younger," Rosa chuckled. "She found herself a cougar."

I leaned closer and whispered. "If Vera's involved with a younger man, she's the cougar."

Rosa rolled her eyes. "I can't keep up with all this stuff."

"What stuff?" Vera asked as she placed the coffee urn on the table.

"Technology," I said, hoping and praying Vera hadn't heard any of our conversation. "They're impressed with your smart phone and texting."

Vera managed a half smile and turned toward Maria. "You must tell Gilda about your meeting with the psychic."

I turned my attention to Maria, who appeared delighted to share her morning adventures.

"She agreed to take one hundred and twenty dollars in cash." Maria frowned. "We had to pay upfront."

"That was a mistake," Rosa said. "We should have suspected something was fishy when she took her time rolling those bills and tucking them away in her purse."

I could easily imagine this scene. Maria and Rosa must have worn down the psychic, who feared they wouldn't pay if they weren't satisfied with their readings.

"She got some things right," Maria said grudgingly. "She saw all my kids."

"But not mine," Rosa said. "She saw three sons but no daughter."

"She talked a lot about our journeys across the ocean and all the obstacles we've had to face throughout the years." Maria rolled her eyes. "I didn't need a psychic to remind me of the hard times."

"She kept showing us a picture of a boat," Rosa said. "And telling us we needed to be more open and courageous. I'm almost eighty years old. I've shown enough courage for two lifetimes."

"What she predicted about the future is so—" Maria turned to Rosa. "I've been thinking about it all afternoon."

"Just forget about it," Rosa said. "We threw away money."

"What did she predict?" I've had several readings, and while most of the information was generic, there were kernels that later proved to be true.

"She told us we would be spending most of the winter and spring planning a special feast," Maria said. "She could see us huddled over our smart phones, texting and meeting with friends to plan this feast. Traveling and baking for weeks on end."

I decided not to mention anything about the smart phones. The psychic had assumed—incorrectly in this case—that Maria and Rosa, like most other people, depended on their smart phones. "Well, you do like to bake. And between the two of you, there's at least one family celebration each season."

"Shannon's confirmation?" Rosa said. "That's the only event I can think of right now." She pointed her chin at Maria. "Unless Belinda gets married."

"Even if she meets someone this week, there's no way she'd get married that quickly," Maria said.

"Unless she eloped," I added, hoping to insert some humor.

"Bite your tongue!" Maria shuddered.

"If she eloped, there wouldn't be any need for a

feast," Rosa said.

"Enough about elopements!" Maria appeared rattled. "We got taken by that witch. I wish I knew who I could complain to." She looked at Vera and me imploringly.

"Her name is Priscilla," Rosa said as she reached for her purse. "I've got her card somewhere." Muttering to herself, she rummaged in her purse and finally located the card. "Priscilla Tremaine."

Maria grabbed the card. "I'll ask Belinda to go to her website and complain. Write one of those bad reports, so other people won't be swindled by her."

Priscilla. The name sounded familiar, and then I recalled my conversation with Cassandra. Priscilla must be her mentor, the woman who has been guiding her psychic journey. I started to share this morsel and then realized it wouldn't help matters. Glancing over at Vera's stricken face, I realized she had also made this connection.

"Forget about it," Vera said. "What's done is done." She pointed to my watch.

Ten to seven. I'd have to rush if I wanted to make the séance on time. I rose and hugged the women goodbye.

Chapter 22

I arrived just before seven o'clock. But I wasn't the last arrival. Leo came several minutes later, managing to appear both annoyed and extra hot. Unlike the previous evening, he had dressed up for tonight's séance. Black pants with a royal blue cashmere pullover. Was he going out afterward?

Kaitlin giggled and nudged me. "Did you plan your outfits ahead of time?"

Sure enough, we were dressed in the same colors. I felt myself reddening while Leo managed a smile and winked at me.

Everyone else in the room appeared subdued. Cassandra and Jake sat next to each other; their heads close together. Adam had his arm around Hannah who nodded but said nothing while Adam whispered in her ear. Daniel and Bob were playing with their smart phones.

Cassandra rose. "It's time."

Everyone got up and followed her into the dining room. No one spoke, but there appeared to be a general air of distraction, of wanting this all to be over.

I couldn't have agreed more. After hearing about Maria's and Rosa's psychic experience, I felt less confident about Cassandra's ability to solve Sarah's disappearance. My skepticism had increased tenfold. I wondered if I should out myself and leave.

Cassandra liked the number of participants to be a multiple of three. If I left, two other people would also have to go. And that would mean Cassandra and Leo would have to decide which participants were most likely to be involved in Sarah's death.

Jake and Leo were at the top of my suspect list, followed by Hannah. A surprising third, but after what Kaitlin had shared about Sarah's promiscuous behavior, I could imagine Hannah stepping up to ensure her man was safe from another woman's clutches. Hannah would want to dump the man, not have him lured away.

While Kaitlin's husband was also propositioned, I couldn't imagine Kaitlin seeking a private rendezvous with Sarah. Kaitlin was up-front about everything—she had already reprimanded Sarah, and unless Sarah continued to pursue Wayne, there would be no need to take further action.

Daniel and Bob. What could be their motivation? I assumed they didn't respond to Sarah's overtures. But if they did? Again, I had no way of knowing and couldn't dismiss them as suspects.

Adam. Dear Adam. While he and Sarah were close in elementary school, they hadn't continued their relationship past Grade Eight. Sarah had moved on with her fringe group. Who had Adam pursued? Neither Kaitlin nor Hannah mentioned his past. He had shared his university experiences and relationship with Teresa—the Italian girlfriend who had hoped for a marriage proposal. But now, involved with Hannah and hoping for a long-term relationship, I doubted Adam would be interested in pursuing Sarah. But maybe, for old time's sake?

"Gilda, are you coming?" Leo waited at the door

for me, his eyes deep with concern.

"Sorry! I have a habit of wool gathering." I was embarrassed to be still standing outside the room. I followed him inside.

Jake was lighting the nine candles that surrounded another freshly-baked loaf of bread. In spite of the carb-laden meal I had consumed, I craved a slice. I wondered what Cassandra did with the bread after each séance. Did she and Jake freeze it for later? Or throw it out?

Glancing around the room, I noted the change in seating plan. Cassandra was still sitting at the end closest to the door. To her left sat Kaitlin, then Hannah and an empty chair I assumed was my spot. Across from me sat Bob, to his left Daniel, Adam, and Jake. Leo's place was at the far end, directly across from Cassandra.

"We shall begin," Cassandra said in a low, confident voice. "First, I must ensure that all present believe it is possible to communicate with Sarah McHenry. If there any non-believers in the room, please leave now." She paused and waited.

Daniel and Bob exchanged glances but said nothing. I suspect the collective skepticism had risen since last night, but no one dared speak or leave.

Satisfied, Cassandra continued. "We will now join hands and keep them joined throughout the session."

I felt Hannah's relaxed grip. Leo's grip was tighter than last evening's. Again, I wondered about the strength of my grip and if I would be able to keep my hands joined for the entire session.

"Our beloved Sarah, we bring you gifts from life into death," Cassandra said. "Commune with us, Sarah, and move among us."

Several seconds passed, and Jake repeated, "Our beloved Sarah, we bring you gifts from life into death. Commune with us, Sarah, and move among us."

More silence and Jake nodded in Kaitlin's direction. She repeated the summons and waited several more seconds before turning to Hannah, who followed suit. And then it was my turn. As soon as I finished speaking, all the candles went out.

Gasps all around. Both Hannah and Leo gripped my hands. This was a sign from Sarah, one directed toward me. What did it mean?

Cassandra's voice trembled. "Welcome, Sarah. We're happy you could join us. Do you wish to speak?"

Nothing again.

"Leo has a few questions for you," Cassandra said, relief clearly evident.

Was it wise to turn the séance over to Leo? Had Cassandra and I been alone, I would have expressed those concerns. But I couldn't say anything now.

"We miss you and are so sorry for what happened," Leo said, his voice soft and uncertain. "We know you will never return to us, but I...we need closure. We want to know what happened. Please share with us. No one can hurt you anymore."

I could feel more moisture in Leo's hand as it trembled. This was new, uncharted territory for him.

"Were you alone that night?" Leo asked. "One tap for yes, two taps for no."

We waited, but no sound came.

"Ask another question," Cassandra said, her voice almost a whisper. "But leave the response up to her."

Interesting! I had always assumed taps were the preferred form of communication.

"Was someone in this room with you that night?"

More gasps. I wanted to make eye contact with someone, just to reassure myself. But I feared glancing in anyone's direction. Instead, I kept my eyes down, praying for no response. I was surprised by that thought. I didn't want to know, or was I afraid to know? Before I could contemplate the answer, two candles fell with a thud. It was hard to make out their exact location. I wasn't close enough to the center.

"They fell on the bread," Daniel said.

"Continue with your questions," Cassandra said, her voice even fainter.

"Was a woman with you that night?" Leo asked.

No response came.

"Was a man with you that night?" Leo asked, his voice cracking.

A sneeze reverberated through the room. Hannah gripped me even tighter.

"Who sneezed?" Leo asked.

"Uh…sorry," Daniel said, his voice croaking. "I think I caught something at the rink today."

"You shouldn't be here infecting all of us," Kaitlin said.

"She's starting again," Bob said.

"Let's stay calm," Leo said and then asked. "What do I do now?"

"Sarah is still here," Cassandra said. "Ask another question."

Was Daniel's sneeze the answer? If so, was he the culprit? I was confused, and I suspect from Leo's silence he was also confused. But it didn't sound like Cassandra was open to discussing the matter. Or taking back control over the séance.

"Was Daniel with you that night?" Leo asked.

"What the—" Daniel rose and yelled, "All I did was sneeze. Ask Bob, I've been sneezing all day."

"He's right," Bob said.

"Daniel, please sit and join hands with the others," Cassandra's voice rose but still trembled.

Daniel grumbled but sat down and joined hands with the others.

"Can one of us help?" Leo asked.

An interesting question but safer than referring to a specific person. Had I been asking the questions, I would be asking about each person in the room. But maybe that wasn't the best way to conduct a séance. As soon as I returned to Sudbury, I would research séances and see how other psychics handle these situations. Maybe schedule one to communicate with my deceased father.

I felt a cool breeze on my neck and let go of Hannah's and Leo's hands. I gasped and stood. "I…I felt something on my neck."

I tried to make eye contact with someone else—anyone else—but could only make out shapes. Thankfully, someone turned on the lights. I looked up and saw Cassandra standing next to the light switch. "Sarah has left the room." Her shoulders slumped as she turned away from us.

Jake rose and hugged her close as she sobbed softly.

Was she as fragile as Maria and Rosa suggested? I hadn't gotten that impression during our Friday dinner. She had appeared strong and confident, ready and willing to solve this case. But two failed séances and this morning's heckling had taken their toll.

Leo walked to the front of the room and whispered something to both Cassandra and Jake. Cassandra wiped away her tears and nodded. Leo faced all of us. "One more séance, folks. We owe it to Sarah."

Groans reverberated around the room. Daniel and Bob appeared the angriest. And I didn't blame them. They had demanding jobs and young families. Weekends were precious, especially fall weekends.

"Anyone have a problem with ten o'clock tomorrow morning?" Leo asked.

Not as bad as I expected. Whatever the result, I'd be able to leave before noon and still have Sunday afternoon to recover from this trying weekend.

Bob stood and faced Leo. "Do we have your word that tomorrow's séance will be the last one, regardless of the outcome?"

Both Cassandra and Leo nodded.

Daniel and Bob were the first out the door. Adam approached Hannah and whispered something in her ear. Hannah's facial expression was difficult to read. She didn't appear thrilled with Adam's suggestion, but she did follow him outside. Cassandra had disappeared. Jake and Leo were deep in conversation.

Kaitlin turned to me. "Another bust. I'm glad Bob forced the issue with Leo. I'll have to miss church tomorrow, but at least this will be over." She glanced at her watch. "The girls should be in bed by now. I hope Wayne started the fire." She winked at me and left.

Leo waved and headed out. There'd be no after-séance meet-up tonight.

Chapter 23

Alone on a Saturday night in Parry Sound. Déjà-vu all over again. During those seven months, I had spent many weekends alone. My parents and friends would call, urging me to visit, but I always had a ready excuse: *A storm is on its way. I have mountains of marking. This yearbook project is taking over my life.*

Sarah's yearbook. I had forgotten all about it. I took it out once more and reread all of Sarah's poems, even the silly ones about butterflies, balloons, and sticky candy. As I read each page, I hoped and prayed for new insights. It was clear Sarah wanted me to help solve her murder. The cool breeze during the séance had come from somewhere, but all the doors and windows were closed. The supernatural was the only possible explanation. I turned to the two-page autograph spread and reread each message, searching for clues. But there were no hints of innuendo or anything that could be construed as inappropriate. These were light, often humorous comments from well-adjusted thirteen- and fourteen-year-olds. But one of those well-adjusted teenagers may have killed Sarah.

I turned to the last page and stared at the graphic. Forever and a Day: I had inadvertently introduced the expression to them. While planning the music for the Grad Dance, the students shared their favorite songs. Daniel asked for my preference. Without thinking too long, I blurted out, " 'I'll Never Find Another You,' by the Seekers."

"Who?" Several voices asked. I hummed the melody and sang the second verse of the song. I mumbled through the verse about everybody finding the right person, but the only words I was sure of were "But I know I'll never find another you."

Intrigued, the students wanted to hear more. Not trusting myself to remember all the lyrics, I chatted about the Australian folk band that had garnered a large following during the 1960s and 1970s. Whenever I mentioned those decades, the students perked up. While I had been born in 1960 and had been too young to visit Woodstock or participate in rallies, I still managed to capture their interest with second-hand recollections of the period.

Unfortunately, the song also conjured up bittersweet moments. When Luigi and I planned our wedding, we had to pick a song. After spending a week listening and rejecting songs, we finally agreed on "I'll Never Find Another You."

After our breakup, I resolved never to listen to it again. And then I let it slip that it was my favorite song. Those last two weeks of June, the students talked about it incessantly. Hannah brought in an old turntable and a battered Seekers album from her parents' collection. I had to listen to the song each day. And several times during the Grad dance.

I needed a distraction; any distraction would do.

Nine-fifteen. It would be six-fifteen in Vancouver. I cursed the three-hour difference that separated Carlo and me. Soon—very soon—we would have to discuss geography. All of Carlo's family lived out west. My mother lived in Sudbury. Could we achieve a compromise?

I considered what Vera had shared. With my mother spending her winters in Italy, I might be open to spending a month or two in British Columbia. Any longer would require a difficult decision about ReCareering. Was I ready to hand over the reins to someone else or close down the office?

I picked up my phone and scrolled through the list of numbers. Adele. Jenny Marie. Laura. If any of them happened to be home, they would suggest meeting up for coffee or drinks. And then I would have to explain what I was doing in Parry Sound. As I scrolled further, I noticed Jim Nelson's name. I hit speed dial and waited. Would he be home on a Saturday night?

One. Two. Three. Four rings. "Hello," Jim's rasping voice sounded close. And somewhat reassuring.

"Jim, it's me, Gilda."

"Ah, yes." He sounded a bit off, as if he had just awakened.

Tempted to tease him about going to bed early, I decided it would be best not to cross that line. Light banter was fine, but too much familiarity could create awkwardness in the future. "I hope I'm not disturbing you. I had an eventful day—"

"Hold on a minute," Jim said. "I'm going to record this conversation."

Hmm. He had never recorded any of our earlier conversations. But then all our previous telephone conversations had been short and to the point. Anything longer had occurred in his office. Had he recorded those conversations? I decided not to ask. Instead, I described each of the day's events, starting with the Holistic Fair.

I left out my encounters with Maria and Rosa at the fair and briefly mentioned the dinner at Vera's.

Jim whistled. "Lots of meat there. Now, we have to figure out how to cook it." He added. "You must be beat."

"Not really." If anything, I was so wired, I knew I wouldn't get much sleep. I still had to deal with Carlo's call later this evening. He wouldn't be happy to hear about two failed séances and a third one scheduled for tomorrow morning. But nothing would come of it. Sarah might appear again, but I doubted she would send decipherable messages. I wondered if she would respond better if I asked the questions.

When I suggested this to Jim, he said, "I'd stay out of that hornet's nest. You're not a psychic or a trained police officer. Even if something did emerge, a lawyer could contest it later."

"A lawyer?"

"You better believe it." Jim chuckled. "If an untrained person conducted a séance where I was targeted, I'd make sure I had a lawyer on speed dial."

"I can see that happening with those two."

"Spill it, Gilda."

"Jake Coburn and Leo Mulligan."

"You'd better have lots of proof if you're going to play with those two and their lawyers."

"Just gut feelings I'm having."

"They're both ladies' men," Jim said. "Does that have anything to do with it?"

"Yes…no…it's more than that." I paused. "I'm convinced they both responded to Sarah's overtures."

"You're convinced the others didn't?" Jim asked. "If this woman was as attractive as you say she was, I think most red-blooded men would be tempted."

"But they wouldn't act upon it," I said. Bob and Daniel may have cast admiring glances toward the Barbies, but other than strolling around the room they did little about it. They were married men, who at some point had figured out how to handle women. Adam did go out with Sarah in Grade Eight, but he had Hannah now. I believed him to be a one-man woman, unlike Jake, who liked to play the field. As for Leo, I was tempted to believe Ann McHenry, who had nothing good to say about him.

"As far as I'm concerned, there are eight suspects. And I'm not prepared to dismiss any of them."

I gasped. "You're including Cassandra?"

"Yep."

"What could be her motive?"

"You just shared it," Jim said. "Sarah put the moves on Jake, and he responded. This could be a case of the scorned woman."

"Jake would never leave Cassandra."

"Not even if he had two million in the bank?" Jim asked. "You keep forgetting about the tidy nest egg Margaret left her kids. It's hatching soon."

"Jake and Sarah? It's not…I never thought…"

"Cassandra's your pet, and you want to see her happy," Jim said. "And so is the other Coburn."

"Adam." I had hoped to meet up with him, but it hadn't worked out. Maybe tomorrow morning, I'd drop by and surprise him at his father's house.

"Yeah, those two. I can hear it in your voice, Miss Greco. I suspect your students also heard it all those years ago."

"What happens now?" I didn't want to get into a

conversation about favoritism. Had I been that obvious? And what about the other two decades of my career? I couldn't recall a single student suggesting favoritism.

"Go to bed early. Tomorrow morning, have a decent breakfast and go to the séance. I suspect it'll be another bust. Afterward, hop in your car and drive back to Sudbury. Take the rest of the day to relax and give me a call Monday morning." Jim paused. "Before leaving, I recommend you give the yearbook and poems to Leo. It's evidence, and it shouldn't be tampered with." He let out his breath in disgust. "I suspect it may already be contaminated."

"Mrs. McHenry doesn't want Leo to have it." I didn't care for his comment about contamination.

"Possession is nine-tenths of the law. It's in your hands now, and you should do the right thing. A graphologist needs to examine all those autographs and compare them to the calligraphic letters."

"But there's no connection." I flipped through the pages. "The cursive writing is all over the place—block letters, different slants, hearts, colored markers. And the calligraphic letters are bold and upright."

"Trust me, a graphologist will find something." Jim yawned. "Gotta go. I've had a long day, and I think I'm coming down with a cold."

"Thanks, Jim," I said as I heard the phone click.

Chapter 24

I heard the ping as soon as I hung up. I checked and found a text from Kaitlin:

—*Forgot to mention…Hannah found Sarah's yoga DVD. Come over tomorrow at 9. We'll watch and chat.*—

I groaned at the thought of another morning meeting. I had planned to sleep in, have a leisurely breakfast, pack my bag, and check out of the hotel before going to the séance. Why couldn't they have shared earlier? I could have watched the DVD tonight and maybe found some clue.

Five to ten. It was still early enough to drive to Hannah's place, or maybe she was at Adam's. I wondered about their "at-home" dates. They would have to coordinate with their respective parents. Or maybe not. The man whore might not be spending his Saturday nights at home. Either way, I would have to intrude. Or perhaps Kaitlin had the DVD. No way was I disrupting her Saturday night with Wayne.

The telephone chimed Carlo's ring. I took several deep breaths and answered.

"Hello, bella." He sounded happy and relaxed. And now, well now, I would have to disrupt his happy mood.

"Hi, Carlo. How are you?"

He lapsed into another travelogue about the joys of

West Coast living. I let him speak, all the while thinking of how I could put a positive spin on the last twenty-hours in Parry Sound. In the seven months, I had lived here, I didn't recall ever having had such an eventful weekend.

At some point, I must have zoned out of the travelogue.

"Gilda! Are you still there?" Carlo chuckled. "I must be overdoing it."

"A bit," I said, joining in the laughter. "We'll talk about spending more time out west when you come home."

"Really?" He sounded surprised but happy.

"Yes," I said, realizing I was starting to imagine myself out there. Not permanently, but for enough time to please Carlo. And, at some level, I was also hoping he would maintain that happy mood when I shared my own weekend experiences.

"I…uh…did check out some properties in Kelowna and Victoria," he said.

"You did, eh?" Kelowna was a three-hour drive from Tania's house in Vancouver, while Victoria was a three-hour ferry ride away. Too far for daily visits but definitely doable on weekends.

More laughter followed. This was perhaps our most mellow conversation in weeks. Why had there been so much tension lately?

Tania and the divorce. She had not been happy with her ex-husband's lawyer, who pushed for shared custody, a situation that could only occur if she and the kids moved back out west. And Carlo was even less thrilled with them moving back west. During the year Tania had lived in Sudbury, he would drop over at least once each day.

"How did the séance go?" Carlo asked.

I retold the events of the last twenty-four hours, skimming over details of my encounters with Leo Mulligan and my phone calls to Jim Nelson.

Carlo swore under his breath. "I can't believe Mulligan is continuing with this...this farce." He paused. "I had some time this afternoon and decided to do my own investigating into Sarah McHenry's death."

I sat up, fully alert to the conversation.

"OPP ruled it an accidental death. The woman had been seen leaving the bar alone and in an inebriated state."

"She could have been meeting someone." I wondered which bar she had visited and how far away from the place she died.

"There were no traces of another person or car near her body."

"So, what's your theory?"

"I'd go along with the OPP report." He groaned. "Something Mulligan has refused to do. He's gone rogue, you know."

"What?"

"I don't think his colleagues know what he's been up to this weekend. And I don't think Sarah's parents would be too thrilled to learn he has opened up the investigation. I gather they agree with the OPP's report."

Maybe Mr. McHenry did. That might explain his wariness when he saw me at their house this afternoon. As for Leo, he had gone public when he reprimanded the young waitress this morning.

I felt the need to defend Leo. "He's assured us that

tomorrow's séance is the last one."

"And what happens afterward?" Carlo said. "Will you be able to let this go?"

He had my number down pat. And now—well, now—I had to level with him. "I've hired Jim Nelson for the week."

"Nancy Drew and Nelson. Why am I not surprised?"

"I owe it to Sarah's memory," I said.

"And you're feeling even guiltier now that she's sent you a sign from above."

"I felt that cool breeze on my neck," I said.

"You could have been sitting near a vent." He added, "If I had been there, I would have checked the ceiling and walls. And I would have gone around the table, asking the psychic, Sarah, or the power on high about each person in the room."

He would have been more thorough than Leo. I was still smarting from Leo's quick departure. I had hoped for reassurance from him, or perhaps something more. I wondered about his possible guilt and his date for the evening.

Part of me wanted to share my suspicions about Leo, but I hesitated. Knowing Carlo, he would not hesitate to contact Leo's superior and recommend that Leo should terminate the investigation. When I was one of the prime suspects in the Murder of the Four Blondes, Carlo had steered clear of any involvement with me. In our private telephone conversations, he had mentioned having dinner once the investigation was over.

"I should be there," Carlo muttered.

Yes, you should. Had Carlo been in Sudbury, he

would have accompanied me to Parry Sound. But I doubt he would have been allowed to participate in the séance. Or maybe he would have insisted. I tried to imagine a conversation between the two alpha men. As for co-operation, I doubt Carlo would have agreed to participate in a second or third séance.

"I'm leaving right after the séance." If Kaitlin or any of the others suggested lunch, I would plead a previous commitment. Thoughts of Adam sprang to mind. I would extend my invitation once more and leave the ball in his court. Friday evening, he had sounded enthusiastic and shared the invitation with Hannah. Had Hannah's indifference rubbed off on him? She appeared more than willing to hop down to Florida during Christmas break, even if it meant being away from her family during the holidays. All that seemed to matter was Dougie and, of course, Jake. I suspect Adam was a distant third in her affections.

"Well, at least Maria and Rosa are there to make sure you don't get into too much trouble." Carlo laughed. "I would love to have been a fly on the wall during their psychic readings."

I laughed, relieved at the change of mood. As for Maria and Rosa, I was happy to hear they would be leaving before the séance. Neither one of them would dream of missing a christening or any other special family event.

"I'll call tomorrow," he said as he hung up the phone.

While I wondered at the abrupt end to our conversation, I was glad we had ended on a more positive note. I hoped he would call after the séance. It would end around eleven o'clock tomorrow morning—

eight o'clock on the west coast. For the past two weeks, I had been thinking in both time zones—definitely a harbinger of changes to come.

Chapter 25

Sunday, October 27, 2013

The incessant ringing of the landline telephone startled me. It continued to ring as I tried to focus on my surroundings. For several seconds, I existed in a nebulous plane and did little to stop the ringing. And then reality hit. I was in a hotel room in Parry Sound, not home in Sudbury, and I needed to get out of bed. I picked up the phone and ended the wake-up call that had disrupted my deep sleep.

All I wanted to do was to stay in bed, but I couldn't risk dozing off. Seven-twenty could become eight-twenty and nine-twenty. I could text Kaitlin an excuse, but I would regret not watching Sarah's DVD before the séance. Having read her poems and gone through her yearbook, I had more insight into those last few months. The DVD might connect some of those disparate dots and hint who might have been involved with Sarah.

I recalled Jim's advice regarding the yearbook and poems. I had to admit it was evidence and Leo had to see it. But before handing everything over, I would speak to Mrs. McHenry. I showered and dressed for the day. I hadn't brought any of my yoga clothes, and I didn't feel like doing yoga this morning. Kaitlin had mentioned watching the DVD, not following it. She hadn't said anything about breakfast either. To be safe, I would eat before I left.

I tucked the yearbook into my tote and went downstairs to the breakfast room. As I approached the buffet line, I heard a familiar voice call my name. I turned and came face-to-face with Leo Mulligan and Jim Nelson, an odd couple, and one I didn't expect to encounter in any environment.

What was Jim doing in Parry Sound? And what had he shared with Leo? I thought back to my suspicions about Leo and what I had shared with Jim last night. And then I relaxed. I was paying Jim to investigate, and he would behave professionally.

Both men laughed. Jim shook a finger at me. "We've got to stop meeting like this." In the past, I had often gone to his office early in the morning to discuss our cases. He had once referred to it as our time.

Leo's eyes widened. "Am I missing something here?"

I laughed, and Jim joined in. The thought of us as an item was hilarious.

Jim put a finger to his lips. "Ssh! These walls might have ears, and the news could travel across the Prairie Provinces to the Rockies."

Leo groaned. "Just what I need right now...another call from Chief Detective Carlo Fantin." Leo's eyes narrowed. "You might have mentioned you were involved with him and that he was keeping tabs on this case."

"What?" I couldn't believe what I was hearing.

Jim shook his head. "Your boyfriend was busy last night. He called Leo first and then me."

"What on earth for?" I imagined he had

reprimanded Leo, but what would compel him to call Jim? The two men had not spoken to each other in decades. In fact, Jim could never call Carlo by his first name. It was always "your boyfriend" or "the Chief Detective." And whenever Carlo needed something from Jim, he would send a constable.

Leo raised an eyebrow at me. "I didn't know Fantin was your significant other."

Another person who couldn't address Carlo by his first name. But then Carlo also used Leo's surname. It must be a guy thing.

"He thinks you need extra protection," Jim explained. "We've been instructed to keep a close eye on you."

"And not let you out of our sight until you leave Parry Sound," Leo added.

"That's ridiculous!" I wasn't in any danger. I was annoyed by the lack of progress with the séances and distrustful of both Jake and Leo. I tried but couldn't recall if I had communicated my feelings about Leo to Carlo. And then realized I had not. But I had shared those feelings with Jim.

Leo's fingers drummed the side of his coffee cup. "I don't know what you told Fantin, but he's convinced you're in some kind of danger. He thinks you're getting too close."

"I have to agree," Jim muttered. "Did you bring the yearbook?"

"Ah, yes the yearbook." Leo's voice was stern. "You know better than to conceal evidence from the police." He chuckled. "I gather you didn't share that tidbit with Fantin."

"Mrs. McHenry didn't feel comfortable giving *you*

the yearbook. I'm honoring her wishes." I ignored the comment about not sharing with Carlo.

"Two dates," Leo said. "And nothing happened afterward. I was the perfect gentleman."

"Why does Mrs. McHenry think you're a cad?" While she hadn't used that particular description, I thought it encapsulated her thoughts.

"She had expectations…so did her husband." Leo ran his fingers through his hair and shook his head. "But Sarah…well, Sarah wanted more excitement."

"A party girl," Jim said, his eyes darting between Leo and me.

"And a bit too loose for my tastes." Leo rose and walked toward the buffet line.

Jim leaned over and whispered, "I think your boyfriend may be right about the danger but not the source."

"Stop it!" As I glanced at the half-eaten eggs and bacon on Jim's plate, my stomach grumbled. I should also visit the buffet line, but I didn't want to miss any of the conversation between Jim and Leo. Something had been shared between them, possibly even with Carlo. And they were keeping that information to themselves.

Jim laughed and shook his head. "Not sure which horse to bet on here."

"Too many suspects in the pool," Leo said as he sat. "If today's séance pans out, I'll have to widen the search to include some of Sarah's out-of-town friends."

Thankfully, he had misconstrued Jim's comment. I couldn't resist adding my own twist here. "I'm surprised you've waited this long to move in that direction."

Leo gave me his full attention. "I…we have reason to believe the answers will be found in the séance room."

"From what I hear, that's not going too well," Jim said as he finished eating his eggs.

Leo shook his head at the two of us. "On the surface, it isn't." He turned his attention to the toast on his plate.

I waited for more details, but none came.

It was already eight-forty. I had hoped to pack and sign out before going over to Kaitlin's, but it didn't look like I'd have the time.

"You've got lots of time before the séance," Leo said.

"I'm meeting with Kaitlin and Hannah. We're watching a yoga DVD of Sarah's."

Leo pointed to Jim. "You want to take that one?"

Jim made a face. "You want me to sit and watch three women do yoga?"

We all laughed. Of all the incongruous images involving Jim Nelson, this one took the prize. "You could participate," I said.

Jim shuddered. "That goes beyond the call of duty." He turned to Leo. "Can we trust Gilda with those two women?"

Leo nodded. "Harmless and pretty cats." He shook his finger at me. "Go directly to Kaitlin's place and follow them to Cassandra's."

Visibly relieved, Jim picked up the yearbook and started flipping pages. "Where are the autographs?"

"Last three pages," I said, feeling uncomfortable as both men turned their attention to the yearbook. I felt I was betraying both Sarah and her mother, but I had no choice. Yearbooks were evidence that could be used in a court of law. During my years as teacher moderator, I would start each year by stressing the importance of accuracy on all yearbook pages. I would refer to real-life examples where witnesses had positively identified murderers from their yearbook mug shots.

Leo watched as Jim flipped to the autograph spread. When Jim turned to the page with the graphic, both men frowned.

"What's with the codes?" Leo asked.

As I explained about the song and The Seekers, the men smiled and shook their heads.

Leo took out his phone and started texting. "I'll send these numbers to Cassandra. Maybe she could work them into today's séance. For fun, go around the room asking if anyone remembers their See-ker codes."

Recalling what Jim had said about séances, I was relieved to hear Cassandra would be asking the questions today. But would the participants even remember their codes? When I suggested their memories might be faulty, both men smiled.

"I still remember my gym locker combination from high school," Leo said.

"So do I," Jim said and turned to me. "How about you, Ms. Math Teacher?"

I shook my head. I had enough trouble keeping track of all my passwords and other numbers. The only number I have committed to memory is my Social Insurance Number.

Leo winked. "Remembering numbers must be a guy thing."

"So, you think the men will remember?" I doubted Kaitlin or Hannah would recall those codes, but I could be wrong.

"The geeks will remember," Jim said.

"Daniel and Bob," I said, recalling how difficult it was to pry them away from the computers at the back of the room.

"Isn't Daniel the one who sneezed?" Jim asked.

"Yes," I said. "But there's no way he could...I mean, he's so gentle and..."

Both men shook their heads and smiled. Leo spoke, "Typical of women to think beta men can do no harm."

"They're the ones you have to watch," Jim said. "Especially the beta man who likes to suck up."

Leo's eyes widened. "Which beta man?"

I shook my head at Jim. Why would he bring this up again?

"Her pet...the soft Coburn boy...the one they called Wannabe Ken."

Leo whistled. "So Ms. Greco has a preference for beta men. Have you shared that preference with the Chief Detective?"

Both men laughed.

Leo pointed a finger at me. "I'd be careful about trusting beta men. They don't always have your best interests at heart." His brow furrowed. "They often disappoint."

Luigi Battista. The ultimate beta man. He accompanied me to lectures and readings and shared many of my interests. He loved to cook and possessed an inordinate interest in home décor. My mother had been so happy I had found a man who enjoyed cooking more than I did. He could spend entire afternoons poring over cookbooks. I should have seen the signs when he suggested spending our date nights selecting china and crystal patterns.

My friends envied my good luck to land such an evolved man. So evolved that he never argued or raised his voice during our time together. Not even when he had to break up our marriage. "I'm so tortured," he kept saying over and over again, not realizing how much he was torturing me.

"Gilda! Are you all right?" I glanced up into Leo's concerned face. During our disastrous date, we had exchanged divorce horror stories. While I didn't recall all the details of his breakup, I imagined he remembered mine. Twenty-one years ago, not too many people were coming out of the closet and breaking up marriages.

"I've got to go," I said, rising and picking up my jacket. "See you at Cassandra's." I turned to Jim. "What are your plans?"

He shrugged. "I'll be tailing you to Sudbury."

What a waste of time! I would let Carlo know when I called later.

Jim turned back to the front of the yearbook. "I'll go through each page of this book."

"Each page?" I had glanced at the first few pages and the autograph pages. I realized now that the other pages could also contain scrawled comments. The students liked to mark up wherever they appeared in the book.

"I'm thorough," Jim said and turned to Leo. "Do you want to stay here or—?"

"Let's finish breakfast and go over to my office," Leo said.

Breakfast! I realized I hadn't eaten a thing. Seeing Leo and Jim had thrown me. Part of me was annoyed by Carlo's high-handed behavior. Another part reluctantly welcomed his concern. I wondered which of my comments had triggered him. I had shared much more with Jim, who didn't appear to share Carlo's concern. If anything, he was annoyed to have been ordered to protect me. As for Leo, he appeared more amused, but then he hadn't gotten up early and driven ninety miles to follow me around Parry Sound.

Chapter 26

I arrived at Kaitlin's several minutes late, filled with a ravenous hunger that had overtaken me. So preoccupied with the sudden appearance of Leo and Jim, I had only sipped half a cup of coffee while the men had eaten their breakfasts. Why hadn't I gotten up and helped myself to a muffin or something more substantial?

Two little girls greeted me at the door.

"You must be the teacher," the smaller one said.

"Her name is Ms. Greco," the taller one said, poking her sister. "Don't you remember what Mommy told us?"

Meanie resurrected in the older child. As for the younger child, she appeared on the verge of tears. I knelt down and hugged her. "What's your name?"

"Bettina." Barely a whisper but a hint of a smile.

I turned to the older child, who thrust out her hand. "Rachel."

"Lovely names for two lovely girls."

A tall, lean man appeared behind them. Definitely a beta man, I couldn't resist thinking. It would make sense for an alpha woman to seek someone more laid back. And Kaitlin had found him in this handsome man with twinkling hazel eyes and a warm smile.

"Wayne Grant," he said, holding out his hand.

"Gilda Greco." I was surprised by the strength of

his grip. Maybe not so beta after all.

Kaitlin appeared, followed by Hannah. Both were dressed in sweats and wearing minimal makeup. I was surprised to see bags under Hannah's eyes and a general listlessness in her movements. Kaitlin's demeanor was also subdued. The past two days had taken their toll. I imagined both women looked forward to getting back to their lives.

"We're all set up in the family room," Kaitlin said.

I followed the two of them inside to another beautifully decorated but functional room. More of the blue color scheme but less bric-a-brac. I was happy to see a teapot, a basket of assorted muffins and croissants, and a fruit platter on the coffee table.

We sat on the sofa across from the television. Hannah moved closer to the screen. "We taped this segment a week after Sarah arrived. It was supposed to be the first of five segments Sarah planned to send to a producer." Hannah sighed. "She hoped to have her own yoga show on television. Or maybe create a DVD and sell it."

"So many pipe dreams," Kaitlin said, shaking her head. "Each week, she'd come up with a new moneymaking scheme. She'd start planning and lose interest within days. If she had stuck with even one of those schemes, she might have been successful."

I wondered about the other schemes but before I could ask, Hannah pressed PLAY. I watched, mesmerized, as Sarah went through a Hatha yoga routine. I listened as the familiar voice described each step in detail and gave encouragement along the way. Toned and tanned, she appeared at least ten years younger than her thirty-five years. And she looked younger and prettier than both Kaitlin and Hannah.

It would not have been easy to be Sarah's friend. But the men of Parry Sound would have had no problems befriending the blonde bombshell. "When did she start having problems?" It must have been heartbreaking for the McHenrys to watch their lovely daughter fade and then disappear right before their eyes.

"She kept it together until August," Kaitlin said. "That's when I noticed her getting puffy around the face and mid-section."

More clues pointing to a pregnancy. That would explain a lot. But I didn't want to bring it up. I would, however, mention it to Leo and Jim.

"By the end of August, she was a good ten pounds heavier," Hannah said. "And her mood plummeted. She wasn't too pleasant to be around."

"She was still pleasant enough around the men," Kaitlin said, her eyebrows drawn together.

I helped myself to a second muffin. Neither woman noticed. They were both lost in their own thoughts. The yoga segment had ended without providing any new clues. I had hoped to hear more personal comments from Sarah. Was there a way to gracefully leave? My cell phone vibrated. I took out the phone and glanced at the display. Ann McHenry.

"Is there anything wrong?" Kaitlin asked.

"I need to take this call." I started to leave but felt Kaitlin's hand on my arm.

"You can use the den," she said, pointing to the corridor. "It's the last room on the right."

I made my way to the den which, unlike the family room, was cluttered with bags, papers, and other paraphernalia. I cleared space on one of the chairs and sat down. I clicked on the message: "Gilda, if you get a chance, please call me. I...I...please call."

I pressed Redial. Mrs. McHenry answered on the second ring.

"I'm so glad you called back," Mrs. McHenry spoke quickly, her voice a whisper. "I just finished chatting with Eileen, my oldest daughter. She lives in Hamilton and is...was very close to Sarah." She paused to catch her breath. "Eileen wants to talk to you. I didn't want to give her your number without your permission."

"Is she all right with me calling now?"

"Would you, Gilda? She'll be home until about eleven o'clock, and then they're heading out to her mother-in-law's for lunch." I jotted down the number and repeated it.

Nine-twenty. I had time to phone before the séance. "Thanks." I hung up and dialed the number, both nervous and excited about this new development.

Eileen answered on the eighth ring. "Hello."

"Hi, Eileen. It's Gilda Greco...uh...Battista." I hadn't used Luigi's name in years, but I wanted to ensure Eileen would recognize me. I hadn't corrected Mrs. McHenry yesterday, and I doubted Eileen would know of my name change.

"Mrs. Battista, I'm so glad you called." A deep sigh reverberated over the phone. "I've been wracked with guilt since Sarah's death. I had promised Sarah I wouldn't share anything with Mom. And I couldn't bring myself to call the police. But she didn't say anything about keeping stuff from you." A short pause. "She would want you to know."

"I'm listening," I said as my heart pounded and my hands shook.

"I don't know where you want me to start—"

"Start with Sarah's decision to return to Parry Sound." Kaitlin and Hannah had hinted at dark days in Sarah's past. I didn't need to hear another play-by-play.

"All right," Eileen said. "Sarah's bank account had been overdrawn since the beginning of February. I helped her out with two months of rent, and then my husband stepped in. He's a good man, but he felt we were enabling Sarah. We have a mortgage and expenses and, well…I'm working part-time…" Eileen's voice trailed off.

"You did what you could." It must have been very difficult to cut Sarah off, but Eileen couldn't put her family's finances at risk. Nor could she risk upsetting her husband who was paying the lion's share of bills.

"Sarah seemed to understand, but she looked so lost. She was still teaching several yoga classes at a health club, but it wasn't enough to cover all her expenses. I persuaded her to give up her apartment and return to Parry Sound. Mom would let her stay there rent-free. As for Dad, well, she'd have to put up with some of his comments. But nothing more; he's all bark."

I was glad to hear there was no threat of physical abuse. But I suspect the comments of an older, taciturn man could be construed as emotional abuse. I didn't envy Mrs. McHenry her circumstances.

"Everything seemed to go well for the first two months. She got two jobs, one at the yoga studio and the other at the restaurant. She received great tips and started putting money aside. My parents were happy when she started dating Leo Mulligan. He was a bit older and more responsible. He seemed like the perfect match for someone like Sarah. But Sarah didn't agree." Another deep sigh. "She needed and craved drama. And when she didn't get it, she created it."

A common occurrence among people with bipolar disorder. I recall one colleague confiding she couldn't bear the sameness of her life. One thing led to another, and it wasn't too long before her husband left. "What did Sarah do after she left Leo?" Now that I had the facts straight, I felt I could ask this question.

"She found another broken person who also craved drama. And they fed upon each other."

"Was this man free to pursue Sarah?" I couldn't bring myself to ask his name. Was I afraid of what name I would hear?

"Not really," Eileen said, her voice breaking. "But he led Sarah to believe he might be ready for a more committed relationship if she was patient enough."

"Did he provide a timeline?"

"No, he was vague about that and everything else. I told Sarah he'd never be free, but she wouldn't listen." Eileen paused. "And then she got pregnant."

"Oh, dear!" A possible pregnancy had been at the back of my mind. But none of the others had suggested it. And it didn't appear she was pregnant at the time of her death. Leo would have mentioned it.

"Sarah phoned to tell me at the end of July. And then she stopped calling. All my calls went to voice mail, and Sarah was either sleeping or out whenever I called the house. Mom was worried, but I couldn't enlighten her."

"When did Sarah finally call?"

"She called in the middle of August, and she sounded terrible." Eileen's voice cracked. "She had told the man about the pregnancy, and he hadn't been too pleased. He got a bit rough and, well, she miscarried. And then she did a foolish thing. Crying and bleeding, she drove herself to the hospital in Barrie. She didn't want to take a chance someone would recognize her at the West Parry Sound Health Centre. She was gone for a good two days."

"Didn't your Mom worry?" I would have thought Mrs. McHenry would have alerted Eileen, Leo, or someone else in the community.

"It wasn't the first time Sarah disappeared for two or three days. She'd been that way since her teens. Mom and Dad didn't like it, but they got used to it."

And that's why it took three days for the police to find her dead body. No one had reported her missing.

"What happened after the miscarriage?" Kaitlin and Hannah had pinpointed this time as the start of her decline.

"She started pursuing all those men," Eileen said. "Mom was embarrassed, and Dad was furious, but that didn't stop Sarah."

And unfortunately some men like a hot mess! I wondered about the man who had followed Leo. "What about the broken man?" An apt description since Eileen hadn't volunteered any other details.

"I didn't learn his name until much later, and in spite of the one-night stands, I relaxed. I figured she had gotten over him. One night in late September, she called. It was the last time I spoke with her." Eileen paused. "She spoke quickly and didn't make too much sense. When she found out she was pregnant, she stopped taking her meds. Despite my pleading, she refused to start again. She kept telling me she had it all under control." Eileen sniffed. "Sorry, I need to take a minute."

"Go ahead." I glanced at the clock. Twenty more minutes. If Kaitlin knocked to remind me of the time, I would tell her to go on ahead. I needed to hear everything Eileen had to say before the séance.

"Okay," she said. "Where was I?"

"Sarah had stopped taking her meds."

"Right," Eileen said. "When she called me that last time, she sounded high, sky high. And she had this terrible laugh. I had to interrupt several times and ask her to slow down. She needed help, professional help. I offered to speak to Mom on her behalf, but Sarah got even more agitated. In the end, I did persuade her to contact you."

That's when she sent the infamous email. "I'm so sorry, Eileen. I didn't recognize her email address and—" I didn't want to get into my own issues about being addressed as Ms. Battista.

"I couldn't think of anyone else who could help. Sarah had alienated her childhood friends and burned all her bridges in southern Ontario." A long sigh escaped from Eileen. "I don't know how much you could have done. She had already decided to confront the broken man and force him to pay for what he had done."

"What did she mean?" Was she speaking figuratively or literally?

"She kept talking about buckets of money that would wipe the slate clean."

Buckets of money. I knew of two men in Parry

Sound who would soon have access to that kind of money. And they would be at today's séance. I had to ask. "Who was the broken man?"

Eileen whispered his name and hung up.

Chapter 27

My throat constricted as I ran out of the room, grabbed my coat and purse, and rushed out of Kaitlin's house.

"Gilda! What's wrong?" Kaitlin's voice followed me as I closed the door.

I barely acknowledged Wayne and the girls as I made my way to the car. I heard the older girl say, "She doesn't look happy."

I had to see him before the séance and hear his version of events. While I had no doubt the information Eileen had shared was correct, I didn't believe it was damning enough. He had used Sarah and lied to her. He had gotten rough enough to hurt their child. But had he shoved Sarah down that hill? That's what I had to hear from his lips or see in his eyes. Either way, I would know the truth.

I ignored the speed limit and made it to his house in record time. Nine fifty-five. I breathed a sigh of relief when I saw his car in the driveway. He hadn't left yet.

I got out of the car and stood still for several moments, taking in the exterior of the house. Still imposing, but there were signs of neglect everywhere. The driveway needed resurfacing, and the window frames could use several fresh coats of paint. I walked to the door, rang the bell, and waited. No answer. I rang again. This time, I heard his plaintive voice. "I'm coming. I'm coming."

The door opened, and I came face-to-face with an unkempt Adam Coburn. His hair was uncombed, and he smelled ripe, very ripe. I had never seen him looking so slovenly before. In his younger days, Margaret Coburn's influence would have ensured he appear presentable at all times. In the company of Hannah Biltmore, he also made an effort. But from what I saw today, I suspected he let himself go the rest of the time.

His face brightened as soon as he saw me. "I'm so glad you've dropped by, Gilda. I was just finishing up my Secret Sunday brunch." He stepped aside. "Come in. I'll put another batch of pancakes on the griddle."

I made a point of glancing at my watch. "We don't have too much time before the séance."

He frowned. "Didn't you get the call from Cassandra?"

I shook my head, wondering about this new development.

"Cassandra's been throwing up all morning." He snickered. "Either she's got a bout of the stomach flu, or she's finally got a bun in the oven. Right now, the séance is on hold."

I took out my phone and saw the call waiting. I had heard the interruption during my call with Eileen but had forgotten all about it as soon as Adam's name was mentioned. Then I saw the Record button on my phone. Why not record today's conversation? I pressed the Record button and placed the phone in my open purse. I chose my words carefully. "I'm sorry to hear Cassandra's not well. I'll drop by before I drive up to Sudbury."

Adam winked at me. "I want you to try my

pancakes. It's Grandma Coburn's secret recipe that she shared with me before I went off to university. I make it whenever I'm on my own." He lowered his voice. "Hannah would not approve of all these carbs." He patted his tummy. "I've lost fifteen pounds since hooking up with her. More than enough for me." He bowed with a flourish and pointed to his right.

I followed, taking in the general disarray as I walked through the living area into the kitchen. I had visited once before, when Mrs. Coburn invited all the teachers for afternoon tea. Back then everything shone and glistened. But two men living on their own, especially if those men happened to be Douglas and Adam Coburn, would not have any interest in maintaining Margaret Coburn's high standards. "Is your dad around?"

Adam made a face. "He's with Wanda, his latest."

My heart sank at the thought of being alone with Adam. I didn't fear him—at least I hoped I had no reason to fear him. But I was uneasy at the thought of our impending conversation. Would he be forthcoming? And what would be his reaction?

He finished mixing the batter and then focused his attention on the griddle. Always so conscientious when it came to creative tasks. I imagine cooking and baking could be categorized as creative. I winced at the pots, pans, and dirty dishes that littered the counter. He must have had several servings of pancakes. My stomach recoiled at the thought of all those carbs in his system. While he may have overcome his alcohol and drug addictions, he didn't have a handle on his food consumption. Without Hannah around, he could balloon to over two hundred pounds.

As soon as the pancakes were ready, he used a spatula to transfer them over to a nearby plate. After placing the pancakes in front of me, he poured coffee for both of us. Having already consumed two muffins at Kaitlin's, I didn't feel like eating more carbs. But I couldn't disappoint Adam, at least not yet.

I poured some maple syrup on the pancakes and cut a small piece. It was surprisingly good, so moist. "Yum." I decided to block out the mess and stench of burnt bacon—more fats—and focus on the delicious pancakes.

Adam nodded approvingly. "I knew you'd like them. Dad and Jake shake their heads whenever I offer to make pancakes. They think I lack self-discipline." He shrugged. "I'm pretty good most of the time, but Sunday mornings, I indulge."

"What about Hannah?" I wondered if she knew about this Sunday morning secret and what would happen once they married.

"Another martinet," he groaned. "That seems to be my lot in this life."

Had he always whined so much? Thinking back, I remember long conversations where he complained about his mother's endless criticism and nit-picking. At the time, I commiserated and felt for the tortured boy who constantly tried to win his mother's approval. Nothing he did ever measured up to Margaret Coburn's exacting standards. I imagine Douglas Coburn didn't fare much better. Only Jake, the golden son, could please Margaret. And that approval dissipated when he got Hannah pregnant.

"You don't have to stay with Hannah," I said.

His eyes narrowed into slits. "Hannah's the best

thing that ever happened to me. Why should I leave her?"

His mood change startled me. And also frightened me. "It sounds like you couldn't be yourself around her."

"I don't think any of us are totally honest in our relationships," he said, as he stirred his coffee. "Eighty/twenty is more like it."

I found myself nodding in agreement. I could easily apply that ratio to my relationship with Carlo. Even last night, I edited parts of the account I had given Jim Nelson. From the start, I had found it easy to be one hundred percent honest with Jim. But I would never consider having a personal relationship with him. And he felt the same way.

Adam glanced at the clock and frowned. "I hate being left in limbo like this. If Cassandra's not feeling up to it, she should cancel the séance and tell Leo Mulligan where to get off."

"I take it you're not a fan of Leo."

"He's always been a player," Adam said. "Three wives, all those girlfriends. I'd be careful around him, Gilda." He leered at me.

First, Jim. And now, Adam. Had anyone else noticed sparks between us?

"Thanks for the heads-up," I said, forcing a smile. "I'm in a committed relationship back home."

A triumphant smile lit up his face. "Sudbury! I'd like to take you up on your invitation. But it'll be just me. Hannah's pretty busy with her job, and she's saving her vacation time for later in December. She and Dougie are going to some basketball camp in Florida." He wrinkled his nose. "Not my idea of a fun time."

I doubt you were even invited. I recalled how happy Hannah had looked when Jake suggested the basketball camp. Alone with Dougie and possibly Jake thrilled her to bits. The thought came out of nowhere, and I hoped I hadn't verbalized it. Glancing at Adam's face, I saw no change of expression. I needed to respond before he got too suspicious. "Middle of November would work. I'll check the schedule when I get back to my office tomorrow and send you some possible dates."

He nodded. "I'll have no problems getting the time off."

My heart sank at the thought of him arriving and living in my mother's house. Seeing him on Friday night looking so happy with Hannah, who clearly had other interests, had saddened me. I had to tread carefully and not upset him. But I needed to get some answers regarding Sarah.

A phone rang. I checked my bag and then realized it was Adam's phone. He glanced at Call Display and groaned. "Not now." He put away the phone and gave me his attention.

"I'm hoping we can get some closure today," I said. "I can't get Sarah's death out of my mind. Left for dead, exposed and alone."

"She brought that on herself," he muttered.

"Excuse me?"

Adam reddened. "I…uh…mean she is…was a party girl. All those men!"

"You were once very close," I said, watching his every movement.

He made a face. "We worked together on the yearbook."

"You took her to the grad dance."

"I had to go with someone," he said. "Mom kept hinting it would look so nice to have double-date pictures with Kaitlin and Jake." He sighed. "Hannah was going with an older boy from high school, so I asked Sarah."

He had carried this crush for Hannah for a long time. "There were other girls in the class."

He shrugged and said nothing. I could tell he wanted me to leave. But I wasn't ready to go until I had some answers or at the very least, a reaction, to Sarah's death. "I went to pay my condolences to Mrs. McHenry yesterday and chatted with Eileen when she called. So much sadness in that house." A small lie, but I needed Adam to hear the sister's name.

He frowned at the mention of Eileen. "Sarah was broken...always has been. She couldn't get it together, not here and not in Toronto. Coming back was a mistake. She should have tried harder down south."

"I read some of her poems," I said. "She was involved with someone at the end. Someone from the past. Eileen hinted at that when we chatted."

He waved his hand. "I wouldn't read too much into any of Sarah's stuff. She always imagined herself in different circumstances. It was her coping strategy."

"Forever and a day," I said. His eyes widened, and he shifted uncomfortably in his chair. "She wrote that in her poetry." Or perhaps not. I definitely recall seeing the phrase on that last autograph page. But I needed something—anything—that would trigger Adam.

His eyes narrowed. "What are you getting at, Gilda?"

"I think you connected with Sarah during those last

few months."

He took a long sip of his coffee and slammed down the mug. "Yeah, I had sex with her a couple of times. I felt sorry for her."

"I think it was more than that," I said, speaking slowly while maintaining eye contact. "Eileen mentioned a miscarriage."

His face darkened. "It wasn't my baby."

"How can you be sure?"

"I know." He raised his voice. "I want to have a baby with Hannah. I didn't want to have a baby with Sarah."

"Wanting something to be true doesn't make it true." Was I pushing too hard? I had no way of knowing, but I couldn't stop now.

"I'm not your student anymore. You don't get to tell me what I should be doing or wanting." His voice approached hysteria. "For the first time in my life, things were going well. I had Hannah, and I had a job that didn't overwhelm me. When my trust fund comes through in January, we'll have enough to start over somewhere else."

"Does Hannah want to leave Parry Sound?"

"She will," he said.

"What if she doesn't?" I couldn't resist playing Devil's Advocate here.

He shook his finger at me. "Stop it, Gilda. I don't want to hear your negativity." He rose and pushed aside his chair. "I'd like you to leave now."

I could leave and share my suspicions, which were starting to be real possibilities, with Leo and Jim. But that would give Adam time to concoct a story. As for the child, it could be someone else's. Without DNA testing, there was no way to prove Adam Coburn had impregnated Sarah McHenry. The miscarriage had taken place weeks before Sarah's death, much too late for any testing.

If I left now, Adam would call his father, who would arrange for legal representation. People might suspect the worst, for a while. Hannah might even leave him. But once Adam left Parry Sound, the gossip would die down. He could start over somewhere else. And he would if there was even a whiff of a scandal. He was Margaret Coburn's son.

We stared, daring the other to make the first move. I could play this game very well. The Adam Coburn I once knew couldn't and wouldn't.

Adam grabbed my plate and threw it across the room. He threw several other plates, each of them landing well away from me. His face contorted with rage and each time, I could hear him breathing louder.

"Damn you, Gilda! Why did you have to come and ruin everything?"

Chapter 28

"Tell me the truth," I pleaded. "You'll feel much better."

Adam sank into the chair next to me. He put down the dish he was about to throw and buried his head in his hands. He started speaking in a low, muffled voice I had to strain to hear.

"I thought she had changed. She looked so pretty when I saw her on Victoria Day. All tanned and toned in a yellow sundress. I just wanted to eat her up. And so did every other guy at the barbecue." He chuckled. "Kaitlin and Hannah were green with envy. They kept looking at Sarah and then whispering to each other.

"She flirted with me, Jake, Wayne, even Wayne's dad. And later, when we went to leave, she sneaked a kiss. Just a peck on my cheek, but it felt oh so good." Adam focused on the wall in front of him. It was as if he was talking to himself. His voice sounded as if he was in a trance. "I called her the next day and asked her out. She turned me down for Leo. That scoundrel beat me to it. But it didn't last with Leo. He was too old for her. Too much like her dad. She called me the next week, and we got together."

Tears pooled in his eyes. "I wanted one last fling before I proposed to Hannah. I figured Sarah wanted to keep it light as well. Then she got careless."

"You didn't take precautions?" I could hear the

edge in my own voice. What did he mean by "one last fling"?

"She told me she was on birth control. I believed her." He paused. "Big mistake. The night she told me, I lost it. I...I..." He buried his head in his hands and sobbed.

"What happened?" I asked, knowing full well what he would say.

"She kept talking about getting married and settling down in Parry Sound. But I couldn't leave Hannah for her. I never intended to marry Sarah." He glanced toward the living area. "She told me here in my mother's parlor. And then she started to go upstairs to my bedroom. When I tried to stop her, she struggled and fell. Not down the whole staircase but a few steps. She started screaming it would be my fault if she lost the baby. When I put my hand over her mouth, she bit me hard. Thank God, my father was out."

An accident if he were to be believed. I didn't think he intended to harm Sarah or the baby. He just wanted them out of his life.

He continued. "When I didn't hear from her, I figured she'd got the message I wasn't interested." He groaned. "Two weeks later, she dropped by the office. Bold as brass, she sat there waiting to see me. Dad smiled and shook his head. Thank goodness, Jake was out running an errand. As soon as I closed the door, she started threatening me. She told me I was responsible for her losing the baby. I would have to pay if I wanted her out of my life. She knew all about my trust fund, but she couldn't wait until January for the first installment."

"The first installment?"

"She wanted me to give her ten thousand dollars. Only then would she leave Parry Sound and go back to Toronto."

"But that wasn't all she wanted?"

He shook his head. "Once the trust came through, she wanted a monthly allowance."

"Did she specify an amount?"

"It would depend on how much rent she'd have to pay." He shuddered. "I'd have that burden for the rest of my life."

Or her life. I could see a clear-cut motive here. "Did you have ten thousand dollars to give her?"

"I wasn't that liquid. I tried to explain I would need at least a week to get the money, but she wouldn't listen. She gave me twenty-four hours." He banged his head on the table. When he looked up, his eyes brimmed with tears. "I should have come clean and told someone…my dad or even Hannah, but I couldn't risk losing her. So I agreed to Sarah's demands."

I waited as his sobs grew louder and then slowly subsided. He took out a large white handkerchief and blew his nose. "I went there with two thousand dollars. I figured it was enough to pay the first month of rent. But she laughed and threw the money all around. I had to scramble to get it, and all the while she laughed louder and louder. I couldn't take it anymore and I…I…pushed her." He broke down and started sobbing again.

I was out of my element here, torn between two broken young people, one of whom I had cared for deeply. As for the other, she was no longer with us. While I was shocked by Sarah's demands, I knew they were born of an intense need to connect, to matter to someone. Sarah McHenry had lost her child and her childhood sweetheart. Hurt and unhappy, she grasped at the only tangible she could see: Adam's trust fund.

"What are you going to do?" Adam's voice snapped me out of my reverie.

"I think you know what you have to do."

He shook his head. "My life will be ruined."

"You hurt Sarah. You have to own up to your part in her death. I'm sure with a good lawyer—"

He rose quickly, knocking over his chair. I could smell his coffee breath as he leaned over and grabbed my right arm.

"Let go of me," I said as he tightened his grip. Would he hurt me, perhaps even kill me? I had been very fond of this troubled young man, who could be aptly described as a beta male. Leo and Jim would not be surprised by this behavior. And neither would my dearly beloved father. I still recall one of his favorite pieces of advice: *Non confondere la gentilezza con la debolezza.* Do not confuse kindness with weakness.

He hissed, "You owe me, Gilda!"

"What?"

He was so close to my face. I could see the pockmarks from his long-ago acne and a wild, distraught expression I was encountering for the first time. "You led me to believe—"

The doorbell rang. Adam turned toward the clock on the wall. Ten twenty. "It can't be her," he muttered.

Hannah! I breathed a sigh of relief. He wouldn't behave badly in front of Hannah. I would slip out as soon as he opened the door. But he didn't loosen his grip on my arm. Instead, he gripped even harder.

"Our cars are out front," I said in the calmest voice

I could muster.

He smiled. "She'll think one of Dad's friends is visiting."

The doorbell rang incessantly. "What the hell!" Adam let go and walked out of the room.

I picked up my purse and followed.

Adam opened the door barely a sliver. As I approached, I heard him say: "I don't know who you're talking about, sir. If you don't leave, I'll—"

"You'll do nothing," Jim's voice rang out. "Gilda Greco is here, and I don't intend to leave until—"

"Jim!" I shouted and rushed toward the door. Adam slammed the door shut and thrust out his arm. I felt myself falling and slipping into darkness.

Chapter 29

I awakened to find myself lying fully clothed on a strange bed in a strange room. The room was dark, but I could make out several shadows, and then I heard the soft whispers.

"She's awake."

A deep sigh. "We won't have to take her to the hospital."

"The others will want to know."

I sat up and tried to focus. Two familiar shapes sat across from the bed. Maria and Rosa. What on earth were they doing here? And where was I? "What..."

"Don't speak," Rosa said.

Maria rose and left the room. I could hear a familiar male voice. One I had heard recently. "I must be dreaming."

"No, you're not," Rosa spoke slowly and clearly.

"Where am I?" I asked. "Sudbury—"

Rosa shook her head. "You're still in Parry Sound."

A large shape appeared, and when I looked up, Jim's concerned face returned my gaze.

Fragments of memory returned...Eileen's phone call...Adam answering the door...Adam flipping pancakes...and then, well, the unthinkable. Or maybe it wasn't that unthinkable. "What happened?"

Maria and Rosa exchanged glances and turned to

Jim, who nodded and said, "I think she's ready to hear all the details."

"Start at the beginning," Rosa said, shaking her head. "We've heard all the bits, but now we need to hear the story from start to finish. And so does Gilda."

Maria nodded and went into the hallway. "Meanie!"

"Her name is Kaitlin," I said, shocked to hear that nickname tossed about by Maria and Rosa. If I weren't careful, I would start using those nicknames myself.

Unperturbed, Kaitlin appeared. And she winked at me. If she didn't mind the nickname, maybe I shouldn't either.

"Start at the beginning," Rosa repeated. "We want to get all the details straight."

I couldn't help smiling to myself. The story would be all over Sudbury before nightfall, and across the ocean as well.

Kaitlin nodded. "We had just finished watching Sarah's yoga DVD when Gilda's cell phone chimed. She looked at the number and frowned. I suggested she take the call in my den. She wasn't gone too long, and then she rushed out, pale as a ghost. She grabbed her coat and ran out the door without saying a word." Kaitlin gave me one of her stern teacher looks, one she had down to a tee. She would make an excellent principal. "You should have told us where you were going."

"Or called to let me know what you were planning," Jim said. "You had promised to let me know if you decided to take a detour."

Taking a detour was putting it mildly. What had I planned or hoped to accomplish by visiting Adam? I didn't doubt what Eileen had told me, but I wanted to hear Adam had not tried to hurt Sarah. Or, at worse, it was a tragic accident he sincerely regretted. I wanted to hear the remorse in his voice and a willingness to own up to his involvement in Sarah's death.

Kaitlin continued. "Hannah and I didn't know what to do. We wondered if you had heard from your mother or someone in Sudbury."

Kaitlin turned in Jim's direction.

Jim focused on me. "At ten o'clock, Leo and I started to worry. We had heard from Cassandra and assumed you had as well. We hadn't made too much headway on the case, and Leo suggested I wait with you until Cassandra was feeling better. Leo picked up the phone and called Kaitlin."

"I was surprised to hear from Leo so soon after you left," Kaitlin resumed the story. "I described how upset you looked after the phone call, and Leo sprang into action. He called and checked with Cassandra and Jake, who hadn't seen or heard from you. Cassandra then called Vera, who relayed the news to Rosa and Maria."

"We were about to leave," Maria said. "The hairdresser had taken forever to do our hair, and we were hoping to make it in time for the end of eleven o'clock Mass. When we heard you were missing, we knew something was wrong. If there had been a crisis in Sudbury, we would have heard about it by then. The only other possibility was your mother. We called one of our cousins in Italy, who assured us everyone there was well."

Jim chuckled. "By ten-fifteen, we knew you were still in Parry Sound. I figured you had put on your Nancy Drew hat and decided to investigate."

I winced at the four sets of disapproving glances.

"I phoned to check with Bob and Daniel in Barrie," Kaitlin said. "They hadn't heard from you either."

"Leo put out an APB for your car and I...well I...figured you had gone to visit the beta man." Jim smiled confidently.

"The beta man?" Maria said, turning toward Jim for an explanation that could further delay this conversation and lead to a battery of questions from Maria and Rosa.

Jim waved both hands and fluttered his eyes.

"Another Luigi?" Maria's eyes were slits of disapproval. "Don't you know enough to stay away from men who are...?" She stopped when Rosa squeezed her arm.

"Who's Luigi?" Kaitlin asked. Jim leaned in closer.

While I hadn't shared the details of my disastrous marriage in a long time, I believed both Kaitlin and Jim deserved an explanation. "I was married to Luigi Battista for a year...well, a year less a day. On the eve of our first anniversary, he decided to come out of the closet." I paused. "I guess you could call him a beta man. He was kind, sensitive, and very empathetic."

"But that didn't stop him from deceiving you," Kaitlin said. "Not too empathetic if you ask me."

"You're susceptible to that type," Jim said, softly. "It's why you couldn't imagine Adam Coburn as a suspect."

I nodded in agreement, realizing I still had much inner work to do regarding Luigi and the past. Twenty-one years had passed, but the anger and hurt still lingered.

Maria and Rosa exchanged glances. They still

looked confused and would need more details.

"I'll explain later," I said, knowing that "beta man" would somehow be translated into "loser" by the time I ended my explanation.

Jim continued, "When I saw your car in the driveway, I phoned and let Leo know. I rang the bell and…" Jim's lips tightened.

"He denied I was there and slammed the door in your face." I remembered that much before succumbing to the darkness.

"Adam assumed the door was locked, but it wasn't." Jim's jaw hardened. "I lost a couple of seconds and couldn't stop him from shoving you against the wall. But I did hit him on the head and put him out."

I was still in Parry Sound. But where was I? I glanced around the unfamiliar room.

"You're at Cassandra's place," Jim explained. "The paramedics wanted to take you to the Health Centre, but we talked them into letting us take you here."

"Cassandra's in her room," Kaitlin explained.

"How's her stomach flu?" There would be no need for a séance now, but I still worried about Cassandra. She had appeared so fragile all weekend.

Everyone laughed.

"It'll take about seven months to recover from what she has," Maria said, winking at all of us.

Seven months? And then comprehension dawned. Cassandra was pregnant.

"Or maybe six months," Kaitlin said.

Maria and Rosa shook their heads. "Seven months," Maria said. "Between us, we've had five pregnancies and observed ten more in our children."

"We're experts!" Rosa said.

"I guess I have a lot to learn over the next seven months." Cassandra stood at the doorway, clad in a ruby-colored robe. She appeared pale, but her eyes sparkled.

Kaitlin rushed over. "What are you doing out of bed? You promised Jake you'd take it easy all afternoon. You need to rest, Bella Meatball!"

"Bella Meatball!" So that had been Cassandra's nickname. Half complimentary, half teasing. While I wouldn't have liked that moniker, Cassandra appeared amused, not insulted.

Everyone laughed as Kaitlin shook a finger at me. "Now, who's using nicknames?"

Chapter 30

Within minutes, everyone except Cassandra had left the room. She leaned over and hugged me tightly. "I couldn't bear losing you. If anything had happened…if Adam had…" Her eyes filled with tears.

"I'm okay. Jim saved me." But if Carlo hadn't called and ordered him to shadow me in Parry Sound, I would have fared much worse. I doubt Leo would have reached the same conclusion about beta men. Neither Kaitlin nor Hannah would have considered Adam a possible suspect. How far would Adam have gone to ensure I didn't expose him? Would he have killed me and then disposed of my body?

I forced that thought out of mind and focused instead on the beautiful young woman who sat next to me. "Bella Meatball. Where did that come from?"

"Papa's to blame," Cassandra said, rolling her eyes. "When I was in Grade Six, I fainted in the middle of Phys Ed class. Papa rushed over and, as I was being led down the hallway, I heard him shouting. '*Bella Polpettina*, I've come to take you home.' Someone, I don't know who, translated and afterward I was known as Bella Meatball."

I could easily imagine the scene. Mr. Maddalone beside himself and expecting the worst. As for *Polpettina*, it was a term of endearment in many Italian families. I can still recall one great-uncle complimenting me on my weight gain during adolescence. Thankfully, none of my friends heard him affectionately call me a *Polpettina*. While Adele and Laura would have commiserated, the others would have snickered and tormented me with the name.

My eyes gravitated toward Cassandra's stomach. Soon, she'd have a different kind of meatball, a lovely baby bump.

Cassandra smiled. "I could feel Gilda Margaret this morning."

Overcome with emotion, I shook my head. "You should honor your mother—"

"No," she spoke confidently. "Jake and I have already discussed it. We're having a girl, and we're calling her Gilda Margaret."

"You sound so much like your parents." Both Maddalones had always spoken firmly and resolutely, confident in their views and opinions. But they also considered other points of view.

"Thank you." Cassandra blushed. "They visited me last night and blessed my stomach. They approve of the name as well." Cassandra sat up straighter and made direct eye contact with me. "And now we need to discuss Mr. Battista."

"Luigi?"

"Yes, Luigi Battista, the man who hurt you deeply and altered the trajectory of your life."

I was taken aback by her comment. How much had she heard of the earlier conversation?

Cassandra leaned closer and squeezed my arm. "Maria and Rosa confided the details of your marriage during one of their early visits to Parry Sound. They worried about you and didn't want you sinking into a depression."

"I guess that explains the monthly dinners."

Cassandra shook her head. "My parents would have invited you anyway. I talked about you a lot, and they wanted to meet you." She took my both hands into hers. "You were hurting back then, but you still managed to function. You've recovered, but I still think a part of you won't let Luigi go."

"I have let him go. I haven't seen him in—"

"But you still think about him," Cassandra said. "I believe that's why you ignored Sarah's email."

"What?" I sat up straighter, my heart pounding. When Leo first mentioned the email, I had briefly considered that possibility but then brushed it away.

"It's all right," Cassandra said. "I don't think you could have changed too much. You might have delayed events, but Sarah wasn't meant to live much longer. Her time had come." She glanced away from me, her gaze steady. She had entered the spiritual realm again.

"Did you suspect Adam?" Or Jake, I wondered. While they weren't identical twins, there was still a strong bond between the two brothers. I imagined Jake would be spending most of today by Adam's side. And Douglas Coburn as well. Thankfully, Margaret Coburn hadn't lived to see her son arrested for murder.

She shook her head slowly. "I could feel a negative presence close by, but I wasn't one hundred percent certain. That's why I talked Leo into the séance."

"You made the suggestion?" I had assumed Leo had approached Cassandra and persuaded her to hold the séance.

"When they found Sarah's body, I was on my way back from a psychic fair in Ottawa. As soon as I took the exit, I saw all the commotion and followed the cars to the OPP station. I managed to corner Leo, who was not in the most receptive of moods. I kept hearing 'overwhelming evidence' in the background, but it didn't ring true. Everyone assumed Sarah had fallen down the hill, either accidently or intentionally. I suspected foul play, but Leo wasn't ready to listen."

She paused and then continued. "When Leo found the email on Sarah's cell phone, he started imagining other scenarios. He had some insight into Sarah's behavior, and he also knew what you had accomplished during those seven months you were our teacher. The other constables didn't think the email was worth pursuing, but Leo couldn't let it go. We connected, and that's when I suggested the séance."

I recalled both séances and her strange reactions. "Did you have any suspicions at the séances?"

Her face crumbled. "All I knew was that the murderer was in the room."

"Then why didn't you—?"

"Expose him?" Cassandra shook her head. "I couldn't force the issue. Leo made it clear I had to let events evolve naturally. If it appeared I was badgering anyone, it wouldn't hold up in court." She managed a tight smile. "Douglas Coburn would have hired a lawyer who could run circles around all that 'New Age' evidence."

I thought back to the fallen candles and the cool breeze on my back. "But Sarah was in the room."

"Definitely! And she did send messages to you and Hannah."

"What about Kaitlin?"

"No, Kaitlin just happened to be sitting next to

both of you. Sarah was warning you and Hannah to be careful around Adam."

"So you knew then?" Surely, she could have spared me this morning's encounter.

"No, I'm putting the pieces together now." She smiled. "That's how it usually works. After the fact, everything makes sense. At the time, I wasn't sure who Sarah was warning and who she was hoping to expose."

While I didn't have her intuitive abilities, I felt she wasn't completely truthful. Cassandra had probably narrowed down the suspects to Adam and Jake, something I don't imagine she would share with too many people, not even me.

Cassandra shook her head. "Jake has been faithful to me. There's a lot of gossip out there, but it's all unfounded." She smiled confidently. "I would know if he had strayed."

I could feel myself reddening. Jake had been at the top of my suspect list from the start. I was happy and relieved to learn I had been mistaken all along. Thankfully, Cassandra didn't appear to hold a grudge.

Cassandra took both my hands and faced me. "Now, I want to share a forgiveness ritual with you."

"A forgiveness ritual?" It was the last suggestion I expected to hear. But then nothing had been within the realm of normal since Leo's call Thursday evening.

"Yes, I want to start you off on a daily ritual you can use to forgive Luigi and anyone else who needs it." She paused. "To be clear, I don't expect all those negative feelings to disappear today. But it'll be a start." She stood and took several paces back. "Can you sit up straighter? At home, you can do this in a chair."

I sat up and waited for her next instruction.

"Good, now close your eyes and imagine yourself surrounded by a cocoon of golden light. Let it settle around you, comforting and protecting you with its soothing glow. Snuggle into it and let yourself feel safe and protected by its light." Cassandra's soothing voice calmed and reassured me.

She continued. "Breathe in, inhaling slowly, and let this wonderful healing light fill your heart. Go deep and then slowly exhale as this light expands and infiltrates throughout your body. Continue to breathe deeply until every cell is filled with light."

Five. Six. Seven. I started counting breaths, a habit I had picked up from my yoga practice. To my surprise, I did feel a stretching, an expansion of body parts.

"Now visualize Luigi sitting next to you. He is here to listen only. As clearly as you can, tell him everything you couldn't tell him twenty-one years ago. Share the anger and pain you felt when he shared his news. Say everything you need to say, but do not blame or reprimand him. Only offer the gift of your truth."

I swallowed hard and took more deep breaths. I opened my eyes and turned to the space next to me. I could envision Luigi as he had looked back then. His dark brown eyes, serious but resolute, behind large black-rimmed glasses. His thin lips were tight and unyielding. I swallowed once more and then found my voice. "Forever and a day. I thought our marriage would last that long, but it barely made it to the first anniversary. I know now we didn't have that special spark, that all-consuming love you found with Claude, and I later found with Carlo. But still, I felt betrayed by you. Had you met Claude after our wedding day, I would have been more forgiving. But I struggled with the fact that you maintained relations with both of us over a two-year period. All that secrecy and deception while we dated and even during our engagement year. I couldn't stand to see the happiness and relief on your face as you packed your bags and left. I...I..." The tears streamed down my cheeks, and I reached for a tissue on the night table.

"That's enough for today," Cassandra sat next to me and hugged me tightly. She then leaned back. "Now, imagine two tender loving hands cupped directly in front of you. Visualize them as God's hands and release Luigi into them. Imagine yourself being set free as you release this heavy burden."

I did as she asked and felt lighter. Not completely unburdened, but well on my way to forgiving and finally achieving closure with respect to Luigi.

She nodded. "When you're ready—not today—but sometime soon, you might want to recite the following prayer: 'Luigi, I forgive you for any pain you have brought to me, whether real or imagined, deliberate or unintentional.' "

"Email the ritual and prayer to me." With so much happening this weekend, I knew I would be decompressing for the next week or even longer. But I would also take the time to include this ritual and prayer. I wanted and needed to move on.

Three heavy knocks at the door. And then another large, familiar shape entered. I blinked and glanced up into Carlo's concerned face.

"Gilda," he whispered, his blue eyes leaping furiously as he took me into his arms.

Chapter 31

"Carlo, what are you doing here?" Only last night, he was in Vancouver. Or so I had thought. Had more than one night passed? How had he known to find me here?

"What he should have been doing all along," Maria said, adopting a no-nonsense, take-no-prisoners voice, as she followed Carlo into the room. Rosa, Jim, and Kaitlin followed in her wake. "If it wasn't for Jim, well...I don't know..." She broke off, tears choking her voice.

Rosa hugged her and scowled at Carlo.

I took in Carlo's discomfort and tried to hide a smile. Having been on the receiving end of Maria's and Rosa's praises for almost two years, he was not too happy to be downgraded to persona non grata, while Jim Nelson received all the accolades.

Jim stood there quietly, smiling and accepting the looks of gratitude from Maria and Rosa.

"What about the christening?" My watch and jewelry had been removed, and there was no clock in the room. I had lost all sense of time but figured several hours had passed. It had to be two, maybe three o'clock. Maria and Rosa were committed to their families and, to my knowledge, had yet to miss a christening, confirmation, birthday, wedding, anniversary, or funeral. Trips would be postponed and other commitments broken to ensure the families celebrated together.

Rosa waved her hand. "We'll get there in time for the cake and the opening of the gifts."

They'd have their stories perfected along the way. With their freshly coiffed hair and Sunday outfits, they were ready to waltz in and share my latest escapade, which would eventually be broadcast across the ocean.

"One more thing before we leave." Maria frowned in Carlo's direction.

"Ah yes," Carlo said, taking out a small piece of note paper.

"We should give them privacy," Kaitlin said, winking in my direction.

Maria and Rosa sighed as they followed Kaitlin outside the room. Had Kaitlin not been there, they might have lingered. Jim slapped Carlo on the back and said, "Good luck, Fantin!" As he left, he called out. "Gilda, I'll give you a call later in the week."

Jim addressing Carlo by name. Maria and Rosa following Kaitlin's lead. Something was up. I glanced in Carlo's direction.

"What's going on? How did you get here so quickly?"

Carlo sat next to me. "After our conversation last night, I knew something was wrong. That cool breeze on your neck upset you, and I knew you wouldn't leave until the case was solved. I called Nelson and Mulligan, hoping to find out more. Neither man was too forthcoming, but I did persuade them to keep an eye on you." He frowned at me.

"I know. I know. I should have let Jim know I was planning to visit Adam. But I thought I could reason with Adam and persuade him to turn himself in."

Carlo chuckled. "Still wearing your teacher hat."

I had been wearing it since that first telephone conversation with Leo. In spite of my initial resistance, I had to help solve Sarah's death. I connected with all seventeen students during those short but intense seven months, more so than I connected with any of the other students during my teaching career.

Carlo continued speaking, "I managed to get an early flight and arrived in Toronto at seven this morning, hopped into a rental car, and high-tailed it up here." He leaned over and squeezed my hand.

He appeared extra haggard, and his clothes hung on him. But there was a definite spark in his eyes. He had reached a decision.

"I can't let Nelson be the only hero around here," Carlo said, as he sank to one knee. He took my hand and held it tightly. "Gilda Greco, will you marry me?" I started to answer as he held up a finger and read from the small note. "And attend our *festa* on Saturday, April 12, 2014, in Parry Sound and our wedding ceremony on Friday, May 16, 2014, in Sudbury?"

"Dates already? You know I don't want any fuss and feathers and—"

"Yes or no…I'm waiting!"

"Yes…Yes. Of course I'll marry you, Carlo Fantin." I leaned over and kissed him. "But I don't want a big to-do."

Carlo laughed. "Too late! Maria, Rosa, and Meanie…uh…I guess…Kaitlin have spent the last hour planning all of this. And contacting someone called Priscilla." He frowned. "I'm not certain who she is, but she made an impression on Maria and Rosa. They're going to get themselves smart phones, join Facebook, and communicate regularly with Meanie."

Priscilla, the psychic and Cassandra's mentor. I shivered at just how accurate her reading had turned out to be. With some extra interference from Maria, Rosa, and Kaitlin.

Carlo continued. "The *festa* will be in Meanie's back yard. She's planning on renting tents, tables, chairs, and I don't know what else. As for the wedding, Maria and Rosa have tentatively booked the date with one of their friends at the Caruso Club."

My mind whirled with all these details. While Carlo and I had often discussed marriage, we had never attended to the details. And there had not been a formal proposal until now. The last two years had been busy ones with respect to our careers and the two murder cases.

Carlo smiled. "Your mother will be back in time for the *festa* in April."

"She'll be back long before April." I would have to call before Maria and Rosa spilled all these beans in Sudbury and across the ocean. I would have to persuade Mama to stay in Italy until after Christmas. January was soon enough to start planning.

Carlo held up a finger. "Oh, and they said something about a cougar and her gigolo who would also help. No idea what that's all about."

Cougar and gigolo? And then I recalled the conversation at Vera's house. While I was glad to hear Maria and Rosa finally understood about cougars, I doubted they understood the meaning of gigolo. Where had they picked it up? I was much too tired and overwhelmed to investigate and clarify. I hoped they wouldn't say too much about Vera and her companion when they called the relatives in Italy. I could imagine the shock and confusion that might ensue if gigolo were literally translated.

"You can't let them down," I said, imagining how convoluted the whole conversation must have sounded to Carlo.

"And I won't let you down, ever again." Carlo leaned over and whispered, "I gather there's another unmade bed in Parry Sound."

"The hotel. I forgot to sign out." I had also forgotten to remove the *Do Not Disturb* sign.

"Definitely an omen," he said, taking me into his arms.

Recipes from the Kitchens of
Joanne and Franca Guidoccio

Gilda's Tofu Cacciatore
Ingredients:
1 pound firm, low-fat tofu, cut into 1/2-inch slices
1 cup tomato sauce
1 zucchini, sliced
½ pound fresh mushrooms, sliced
½ green (or yellow) pepper, sliced
½ large onion, sliced
2 cloves garlic, minced
1/8 cup all-purpose flour
Salt and pepper

Directions:
Preheat oven to 350 degrees Fahrenheit.

In a shallow dish, mix flour with pinches of salt and pepper. Dredge the tofu slices in the seasoned flour, turning to coat both sides.

Coat a non-stick skillet with cooking spray and place over medium-low heat.

Add tofu slices and cook until lightly browned, about five minutes per side.

Arrange tofu slices in a single layer at the bottom of a baking dish.

Combine the remaining ingredients and arrange over the tofu slices.

Cover the baking dish with aluminum foil.

Bake for 25 to 30 minutes or until cooked through.

Note: This dish tastes even better if prepared the previous day. Those extra hours give the tofu time to absorb the tomato flavor. Serve over pasta or brown rice. Servings: 2

Cassandra's Baked Tilapia

Ingredients:

4 tilapia fillets
2 egg whites
4 tbsp cold water
2 tbsp Romano cheese
1 tbsp parsley
½ cup melted margarine (or butter)
salt and pepper (to taste)
bread crumbs

Directions:

Beat egg whites, water, cheese, salt, pepper, and parsley.

Marinate fish in egg mixture for 30 minutes.

Preheat oven to 400 degrees Fahrenheit.

Grease a cookie sheet with the margarine (or butter).

Remove fillets from marinade and coat with bread crumbs.

Bake for 8 minutes on each side.

Makes 4 servings

Kaitlin's Vegetable Quinoa Soup

Ingredients:

2 tablespoons olive oil

1 medium onion, diced

2 cloves garlic, minced

1 cup chopped carrots

1 cup chopped celery

1 small zucchini, chopped

10 cups of vegetable broth

2 cups cooked quinoa

Salt and black pepper, to taste

Directions:

Rinse 1 cup quinoa under cold water. Add quinoa, 2 cups water, and a pinch of salt to a medium saucepan and bring to a boil over medium heat. Boil for 5 minutes. Turn the heat to low and simmer for about 15 minutes, or until water is absorbed. Remove from heat and fluff with a fork.

Heat the olive oil in a large stockpot over medium-low heat. Once hot, add the onion and cook until tender (about 5 minutes). Add the garlic and cook for another 2 or 3 minutes. Add the carrots, celery, and zucchini. Continue cooking for another 4 or 5 minutes, stirring occasionally.

Add the vegetable broth. Reduce the heat to low. Cover and cook until the vegetables are fork-tender (about 25-30 minutes).

Stir in the cooked quinoa and season with salt and pepper, to taste.

Yield: Serves 6—8

Grandma Coburn's Pancakes
Ingredients:

1 egg
2 cups milk
3 tbsp white sugar
1½ cups sifted flour
3 tsp baking powder
1/2 tsp salt
3 tsp softened margarine
¼ tsp vanilla

Directions:

Preheat oven to 175 degrees Fahrenheit.

Preheat electric griddle.

Beat egg very well.

Add milk and sugar and continue beating.

Sift flour, baking powder and salt together.

Combine both mixtures.

Stir in margarine and vanilla.

Pour pancake batter onto the hot griddle. Pools of batter should be 2 inches away from each other.

Cook until golden brown on each side.

Place finished pancakes on a heat-proof plate in the oven.

Repeat with the remaining batter.

Makes 12 pancakes

A word about the author...

In 2008, Joanne retired from a 31-year teaching career and launched a second act that tapped into her creative side and utilized her well-honed organizational skills. Slowly, a writing practice emerged. Her articles and book reviews were published in newspapers, magazines, and online. When she tried her hand at fiction, she made reinvention a recurring theme in her novels and short stories.

A member of Sisters in Crime, Crime Writers of Canada, and Romance Writers of America, Joanne writes paranormal romance, cozy mysteries, and inspirational literature from her home base of Guelph, Ontario.

http://joanneguidoccio.com

www.ingramcontent.com/pod-product-compliance
Lightning Source LLC
Chambersburg PA
CBHW070926180626
46817CB00003B/1210